CONTENTS

This book is for Alix: she knows why.

MOSAIC OF AIR

Short Stories

Cherry Potts

Arachne Press

This Edition published in UK 2013 by Arachne Press Limited
100 Grierson Road, London SE23 1NX
www.arachnepress.com
 ISBN: 978-1-909208-03-2
Original UK publication 1992 Onlywomen Press Limited

Printed in the UK by TJ International, Padstow.

Thank you list
Some of the people who listened to some of the stories half finished, or not even started, and in the process helped them get finished, even if they didn't always know that was what they were doing:
Alix Adams, Rudi André, Joyce Cunningham, Tash Fairbanks, Kate Hambrook, Kath Howells, Rosemary Manning, Morph, Ghillian Potts, Debs Trethewey, Lis Whitelaw, Jude Winter.
Thanks also to Muireann Grealy for her proofreading.

FOREWORD

Mosaic of Air was originally published twenty years ago, and some of these sixteen short stories were written as much as ten years before that. They reflect and explore Lesbian life in the 1980s through myth, history, fantasy and science fiction. They reflect my own concerns of the time, which involved a certain amount of marching, campaigning and metaphorical shouting from rooftops. We've come a long way since then, but happily myth and history don't age, and to my delight, neither does my science fiction.

I did wonder whether the concerns and lifestyles depicted in the contemporary stories might have dated, and sometimes I think that I would write these stories differently now, and then I think, would I? Yes, the world has changed - for example, Nina (*Baby Pink/Electric Blue*) would not have been frantic to find a phone box, these days she'd have a mobile. Many of the scenarios played out by characters in the contemporary stories wouldn't happen in the same way, at least not in much of the western world. Alice's enraged cry of 'He couldn't very well marry Philip, could he?' (*Reason to Believe*), is redundant in the UK in 2013; but there are plenty of places in the world where Lesbian and Gay lives are still lived in secret and fear, where these stories would still happen, where standing up for yourself as these characters do could lead to social ostracism, arrest and even death. Women like Rowan still tidy away evidence of their life (*Rowan's Version*), and the un-named protagonist of *Second Glance* is still cautiously searching for clues before speaking to the woman in the bar. Sadly these stories have not dated as thoroughly as I might have hoped. That makes it sound as though these stories are full of doom and gloom, which they emphatically are not. My intention when I wrote them was to explore everything a woman, especially a Lesbian, could be; to test the premise of the Alix Dobkin song, *Any Woman Can Be A Lesbian*, with the passion and humour I found amongst my Lesbian friends and colleagues, and fellow shouters-from-rooftops.

Cherry Potts July 2013

MOSAIC OF AIR

Rhani had finished her work. It was the culmination of a project, the birth of her brainchild. It was the realisation of a lifetime of dreaming and scheming, of five years intense research and hard work. It was also a credit spinner once the trial run was over. There would probably be another doctorate, perhaps a prestigious job at a research station to go with it.

Rhani delighted in her creation. She wanted to show it off, she wanted to keep it to herself. She hugged her delight to her, feeling that she needed nothing more than this perfection of her intellect and skill. She did not need food or drink, and she most certainly did not need Paul. He wanted to be part of her success, but she would not let him. He was not responsible for it. He had even tried to prevent her from spending time on her work. She thought about him with anger in her heart, implacable in her resentment. She was not about to forgive him. Him and his demands, his wanting children before she was too old. This was her child.

For Paul, Rhani's 'child' was a rival.

For the Government it was prestige, and a scientific coup.

For Wilson Avery, it was a career boost, and an honour.

For Cal, it was an escape route.

Rhani's child was a computer, capable of piloting the most sophisticated new ships, and quite different from any computer that had ever been created before.

*

Cal had, due to her inability to stick to the rules, lost her pilot's licence at just the wrong time. She was a smuggler:

she would carry anything illicit from anywhere to anywhere, unfortunately, just when she most needed a clean record, she got caught.

Which was why Wilson Avery was piloting the new ship, not Calista Jerrard.

Rhani had asked for Cal originally, because she was famous, because she was so clearly the best. Then she got busted, shipping political dissidents off their home planet without asking too closely about their exit and entry papers.

If Rhani had ever met Cal she would have despised her lack of education, and she would certainly have considered her business strategies to be little short of criminal.

If Cal had ever met Rhani, she would have thought her an uptight traditionalist.

They would both have been right. They would have hated one another. But they never met. Which is why it happened the way it did.

Part of Rhani's research had been to interview as many deep space pilots as she could find. She had read the profiles kept on them by the authorities, but that wasn't enough. She wanted to know what they most needed from their computers. She had had to keep quiet about some of the responses, and even about some of the things she eventually programmed into her child. She didn't want to frighten her government investors. Cal had not been among those she interviewed, owing to being on a particularly long haul at the time, the one that lost her her precious licence.

However, Wilson Avery had been interviewed. He had impressed Rhani. He was impressive, he worked hard at it. He was also the best pilot available when Cal fell out of the frame.

The trials were supposed to be top secret, and Cal should not have known anything about it. But Cal had space in her blood in almost equal levels with alcohol; she was addicted to the songs of the stars, the silence of the voids between. She couldn't leave it alone. The loss of her licence was the worst thing to have happened to her. She stuck to the pilots' bar like a leech, breathing the atmosphere, drinking the liquor, talking the jargon, longing for the dark outside.

And listening.

So she knew that the prototype computer was finished, knew which company had won the tender for the ship, and when *Astarte* was complete, she heard about it. Later she heard about the medicals and interviews the top guns were getting. She drank even more, trying to dull her frustration. Everyone knew they wouldn't have had to bother with any other pilot if she had still flown her licence. Some of the other pilots doubted she'd have passed the medical. No one suggested that to Calista Jerrard. Cal knew how to use a sonic knife to the disadvantage of anyone stupid enough to look for trouble with her.

And of course Cal knew when Avery was finally chosen. And she knew what the cargo was, even before Avery did. Cal gave up drinking for two whole days.

The cargo was another computer. A huge archive databank for a recently set up colony. The journey was a good long one. Cal craved the dark, the silence, the weightlessness ... the aloneness. And she craved those computers. Her education might be lacking, but Cal had an instinct for computers, for ships, for space. She was a natural with them all. She understood them. She wanted that assignment.

And there was absolutely no way she was going to get it.

Cal reckoned that on a long trip like that she could learn both computers inside out, maybe even tap into the archive and get some culture.

Cal wanted to slice Wilson Avery's smug grin off his face with her sonic knife. But Cal could be subtle when she wanted. And she wanted bad. Bad enough to try anything.

So she was working against time, trailing Avery everywhere he went. Watching his drinking companions, his women.

Planning one hell of a heist. She lived on the excitement of planning. Stopped drinking. Stopped eating, stopped sleeping. One of her ex-friends, she only had ex-friends, observed that she must be in love. Not to Cal. No one could quite believe it.

If Rhani had had any idea what was being planned, she would have had Cal assassinated. Unfortunately she didn't know, and nor did Wilson Avery.

Cal carried a voice encoder with her everywhere, taping everything Avery said. She needed his voiceprint to get through the security. But she also needed to know what the passwords were. And the only way to find that out was to ask him. And the only way to ask him was to get him alone and drug him. And the only way to do that – but Cal was desperate determined.

So if Wilson Avery was surprised when the short dark woman sat beside him at the bar and shamelessly propositioned him, he didn't let on. Cal had noticed he didn't take much time to get to know the women who slept with him, and that there were plenty of them. Of course, if Avery had been less drunk, he might have recognised her. But Cal had been careful. Dyed and curled her hair, painted her face, worn a long diaphanous skirt. Even her best ex-friends would have passed her by without a hint of recognition. Anyway, that was what her research told her Avery liked, and couldn't be much further from how she usually looked.

In the unCal-like handbag she carried her voice encoder, sonic knife and an assortment of drugs, all illegal and of varying degrees of riskiness. She was almost embarrassed at how easy it was, but then she knew the high that comes before a really good contract, and Avery was all set to go first thing in the morning. Or that's what he thought. A few more drinks, and they were heading back to Avery's rooms.

Then a few more drinks. Cal's head was beginning to buzz. She ought to have eaten first. She spiked Avery's drink none too carefully, and hoped the drug would work fast.

It didn't.

Cal found herself having to go through with Avery's intentions instead of her own, found herself being dragged onto the bed. Despite her irritation – she had hoped to avoid this after all – she couldn't help laughing at his attempts to find a way through all the layers of the skirt.

Still she had more drugs – tipping the pin of the brooch that held the scarf wound into her hair. She contrived to scratch him with it, careless of the effect of the mixing of drugs.

Avery's drug/alcohol induced enthusiasm for Cal was overwhelming. He was determined to have her, and thoroughly. He was intoxicated by her; it was a hell of an experience.

Cal put up with it. She was no way going to pretend she was enjoying it. Sooner or later he would be under the drugs and then –

It was later. Cal struggled out from under him and ran for her voice encoder. Her head was unexpectedly spinning from too much drink. She wondered briefly whether Avery had been trying to drug her too. She dismissed the thought. Probably she was just light-headed from success. She ran through all her questions as fast as she could, recording Avery's responses to passwords and codes before his voice started to slur and mess up her recordings. She took fingerprints in resin. She stole his new uniform, his passes, his licence. She liked the feel of that in her hand.

She checked his weight and height, analysed the colour of his hair.

She didn't like the colour his face was going. She coded a medical alert into the door on her way past, and set it to delay long enough for her to get out of the area. Then, cursing herself for being soft, cancelled it. If Avery ended up in hospital before she was on *Astarte*, she would be cooked.

The next few hours were filled with checking the recordings, redying her hair and cutting it, padding out the uniform, building up her boots, making temporary fingerprints. She wasn't too sure how many checks there would be.

Of course she would look nothing like Avery close up, but she wasn't planning on getting close up.

And she didn't.

The first anyone knew about it was when she told them.

Safely out of orbit, Cal disabled the automatic communications system. She wasn't planning on anyone talking to the computer without her knowing about it. She activated the voice encoder and told the computer what she wanted it to do. And it did it.

Cal collapsed with relief. It worked. Somehow she had expected this state of the art computer to have a more sophisticated security system. But then, it did.

Rhani had built in a private channel between herself and the computer that did not rely on the automatic communication channel and would work under any circumstances, short of destruction.

So she knew that her computer had been hijacked.

She was furious. She was also worried, and intrigued. She did not want to alert the authorities yet. She knew what they were like. They'd probably blow the whole ship up, and then where would all that work go? No, she would monitor what was really happening on the ship.

Rhani's corruption from her straight-laced respectability was starting.

She went herself to Avery's rooms. She found him unconscious and barely breathing. She called Paul on their private line. He was a doctor, and although she wasn't sure he would co-operate, she didn't want a med. team who would gossip, so that everyone would know it wasn't Avery on the ship.

Paul protested, but eventually agreed to treat Avery privately. He wasn't particularly confident of a full recovery; it had been a particularly nasty combination of drugs.

Rhani was disappointed. Cal had asked nothing of the computer yet. She had simply keyed in the correct co-ordinates and gone to sleep. Not that Rhani knew that it was Cal. Maybe she suspected it.

Cal hadn't planned any further than getting on to *Astarte*. She had every intention of delivering her cargo. The months of travel would be enough for her to take in the archive, or as much of it as she wanted. She didn't aim to deprive the colonists. She would have to jettison the whole cargo hold to avoid coming into contact with them, but that would be a small sacrifice. She didn't plan on being found out before she had to. The longer she appeared legitimate the better. And it would be a quicker run to unpatrolled space from the colony than virtually anywhere else. After that, there were places for pirates to refuel and restock, she'd manage.

Cal slept for more than twenty hours, and woke up starving. She reached automatically for the food dispenser and keyed in her requirements. The computer hesitated. The false fingerprints were fraying out, and it registered a doubt.

Cal woke up properly, and repeated her order using the voice encoder. The food arrived. She ate quickly, stripping the fingerprints from her fingers as she did so. She instructed the computer to recognise a new set of prints, and placed both hands against the computer's sensor.

The computer sent a message to Rhani asking whether it should accept the new authority. Rhani agreed that it could, and took a copy of the fingerprints. She fed the prints into her own computer. She waited.

A face appeared on the screen. Short, rough, red hair framed a pointed and serious face. Beneath it, an identical set of fingerprints, and the name Calista Jerrard. The information continued, but Rhani was not particularly interested. What she was interested in, was that the best and most dangerous pilot known to several species was in charge of her computer. She wasn't sure whether she was pleased or frightened. In a way it was quite a compliment that Calista Jerrard would go to all this effort to get at her computer – it would have been much easier to steal any other ship.

Once she recovered from the initial shock, Rhani worried whether anyone could have detected her accessing Cal's records. She wondered whether she could risk delving deeper than the basic information that was already on her screen. She read it carefully. She needed to know more about Cal. She called up the list of other files available, most of which were restricted. Rhani thought very carefully about the risks, and decided she needed that information. Using every underhand trick she had ever learnt and then tried to forget, she hacked into the records, and made copies of everything. Some of them were fairly innocuous. Running through the details swiftly, she took in Cal's lousy credit rating with a wince, and felt a little uncomfortable at being party to such intimate information.

She realised that she had already read one file, when she was checking pilot profiles to help decide who to hire for the *Astarte* run. She re-read it quickly. Cal's record was impressive. Rhani smiled to herself, reading it, thinking what a pity it was that Cal had turned out to be a smuggler; she would rather have had her than Avery on this run. Well, she'd got her anyway.

Rhani cancelled the file, and went on to the one she was really interested in; the transcripts of the trial, following Cal's importation of the illegal immigrants. Rhani supposed there were worse things to get caught with, like weapons. She found the transcript difficult to follow, but found a sound recording appended, which was better, although the voices distorted on her machine, which wasn't designed for this sort of thing. She listened to Cal's voice, explaining why she had taken on the refugees, as Cal called them. She made no claims to a political rationale, simply insisting that it made no difference to her why or where they wanted to go. Good credit was all she was interested in.

Listening to the recording, Rhani realised that Cal had not expected to lose her licence. She ran the reel back, over and over, listening to the sudden change in Cal's voice, as she finally understood what her punishment was to be. Her soft, almost insolent tone and the drawl which she used to cover a slight hesitancy, disappeared. Cal's voice became sharp with fear.

You can't do that to me.

Rhani could imagine the change in stance that must have gone with that, she could understand the terror in Cal's voice, and so perhaps, she told herself, she could understand why Cal had stolen *Astarte*. It didn't comfort her much, she had a feeling Cal had nothing left to lose, and would not be careful with her beloved computer.

*

Fully awake and fed, Cal was investigating. She checked out the ship. She checked out the supplies, the cargo. She hesitated over the archive databank, but decided she needed to know the computer that was running her ship more urgently. She also needed to check in on the messages floating around the other ships out there, check whether she had been found out. She wondered if Avery was dead. She didn't much care. She didn't like him any.

Cal went back to the flight deck, checked the messages. Nothing. She sighed in relief. The computer picked up the slight noise, and flashed its ready light at her. She invited it, through her voice encoder to tell her how it worked. The computer obliged, in even tones, and with an explanatory visual display.

Which kept her busy quite a while.

*

Avery regained consciousness, but was weak and confused. Didn't know who had drugged him, some woman. Paul wondered if he meant Rhani. She had told him nothing about why she had wanted Avery kept quiet. It took Avery a few days before he realised he should be somewhere other than in Paul's research clinic. Then he panicked.

Paul suggested that Rhani should talk to him. She dragged herself away from the computer reluctantly.

She was shocked at how ill Avery looked; she had not bothered to check on his progress. She explained what little she could of what had happened. Avery began to look worse. And then he started to cry. Rhani pulled Paul away from the bedside to ask exactly what Cal had given Avery. Paul told her. She was horrified. She began to worry about what would happen to her computer, her concern for Avery forgotten.

Avery surveyed his future. He would never be able to take a ship into space again. Apart from the fact that his reputation would be in shreds when this got out, his health would never fully recover. And he was in debt. Without his lucrative pilot's salary, he was finished. Any wonder that he cried?

*

Cal, meantime, had tired of being instructed. She had slept and woken again several times. She had checked for pursuit, and then idled her way through the recreational facilities. They had clearly been tailor-made to suit Wilson Avery. Cal didn't find they had much in common. She didn't do drugs. Avery apparently had a wide-ranging taste in some extremely bizarre and illegal concoctions. No wonder he had taken so long to react to the drugs she had given him. At least he drank gin. She wondered how he had got the drugs into the perfectly normal dispensary unit. He must have had someone inside the company funding the ship fit it out for him. Actually, Rhani had seen to the drug supply. She had listened very carefully to what the pilots wanted.

It took Cal a while to get used to having a computer that talked to her. She liked it. It was cosy. She could almost forget it was a machine. She spent a lot of time talking to the computer. Computer thought it probably quite liked Cal. It wasn't quite sure how liking was supposed to feel, but it was comfortable with her, they had an easy relationship. Computer relayed this to Rhani. Rhani wasn't pleased. She was jealous of her relationship with her child. She was damned if Cal was going to hijack Computer's affections as well as everything else.

It wasn't until she had run through Avery's entire collection of vids at top speed, that Cal decided to go down to the cargo deck and take a look at the archival unit she was transporting. She spent a while taking the packaging to pieces. Then she played with the controls. It looked easy to use. It would be fun to get at the information, a challenge, more fun than high speed porno vids, anyway. Still, she put it off for a few more days, savouring the anticipation, so that, when she finally returned to the cargo deck, she was almost shaking with excitement. She wanted to get into that information, she wanted to swim in words, the way she swam in the darkness of the starlight, drunk on the whispering of the planets. She was greedy for knowledge, but she was scared as well. Scared of finding out too much.

So she approached the cargo hold in much the same state of mind as she had approached her first ship, or perhaps her first lover. Anticipation, excitement, fear. Cal hesitated for only a second before temptation overcame her qualms. Here was a chance to really submerge herself in all the things she'd missed out on. The training she had received to qualify as a pilot had left so many areas of knowledge untouched, it was so specialised. Physics, engineering, mathematics. Ideally suited to what she planned to do now, she reminded herself. Cautiously she opened the access panel on the library. Because the shippers had not known who would be dealing with it at the destination, they had not voice-locked it. She relaxed a little. Perhaps it would be easy after all. She surveyed the coded lights. Yes it would be easy. All it needed was to be linked to a power source, and into the ship's computer so that she could access the information. She checked the nearest input position for the computer. Not impossible.

She typed in the command on the voice encoder. Wilson Avery's voice requested access to the input panel. Nothing happened. Rhani had, in a fit of pique, instructed the computer not to recognise the command voice. Cal cursed fluently. Computer relayed this to Rhani. Rhani laughed.

Cal decided not to be polite. She cut through the panel with her completely illegal sonic knife. Computer informed Rhani. Rhani stopped laughing.

Cal inspected the tamper repel circuits. She did not think there would be a problem. She wasn't going to try to disable the computer, so it shouldn't react. She pushed the library module into line with the input panel and started lining up the circuits. A soft humming came from the library as it began to receive power. Cal worked methodically and carefully. But she was not sufficiently careful, because she thought it would be easy.

It wasn't. As she adjusted the last connector into position, the sonic knife, which she had thrust into the pocket of her vest, slipped out and fell between the library and the input panel. Without thinking, she leant to pick it up, and her hand severed the sonic links.

Computer triggered the tamper alarm. Cal tried to pull away, and in so doing activated the library. The machines interfaced, with Cal caught in the sonic network between them. The soft humming turned to a whine that grew higher and higher. Cal was surprised that it didn't hurt more, but knew that she had to get it shut off somehow, that the pain would get worse.

She had always been told this was the worst possible thing that could happen to a computer engineer. But the fact remained that she couldn't get her arm out of the mass of sonic waves. She twisted frantically to see if she could reach the knife, but it was just out of reach. She couldn't stretch far enough to get her fingers to the input panel to shut it off. All she could reach was the library, which was busy loading its information into the ship's computer, which wasn't what she wanted. She hit the off switch, but nothing happened. She was beginning to feel dizzy and frightened. The noises spiralled in her head, and she could no longer see straight. Her arm was going numb and she was shaking. When she could bear it no longer, she gave in to the shaking in her limbs and passed out; falling through the sonic circuit, catching in it like an insect in a spider's web.

Computer could scarcely contain the data that the library was pouring into her memory. She wished Someone would turn it off before it overloaded. She sent another distress call to Rhani, and then the pilot fell into the network.

It was like nothing Computer had ever received before, her circuits reeled under the impact, and her fail-safe triggered. The input panel shorted out. The pilot hit the floor.

Computer assimilated the data she had received and sent a damage report to Rhani.

Circuits: Minor short in cargo bay.

Structure: Some damage to panelling input point 07 cargo bay.

Memory: Intact.

Pilot: Unconscious. Bruising to left knee and shoulder, left cheekbone. Cut to left hand. Considerable sonic disruption to nerve structure whole of left arm. Estimate will regain consciousness within three minutes twenty-two seconds.

Rhani acknowledged the report. Computer readied the necessary equipment in the med. deck and waited for Cal to wake up. While she waited she reviewed the information she had been force-fed. She got a shock.

Along with the archive and culture package from the library, she had all Cal's memories.

This had a pretty devastating effect on her programming. For starters, she didn't tell Rhani what she had received. She gloated, she plaited her wiring in excitement, she wondered how the hell to use what she now knew. She started thinking in slang. She decided not to let on to Cal that she knew her inside out. Cal might find the real off switch and kill her.

*

Cal regained consciousness with an empty feeling in her head, the metallic taste of blood in her mouth and a soon to be empty feeling in her stomach. She vomited. Computer set the suction cleaner. Cal drew a difficult breath, and decided she wasn't going to die. She seemed to be wedged between sheets of metal. She tried to get to her feet. Her left arm wouldn't move. A voice from somewhere above her told her that she had fallen into a sonic web, and to move very slowly. The empty feeling went away and her brain flooded with distress like the howling of cubs who have lost their mother. Never one to restrain herself, Cal howled.

Damn sonics. Why in hell can't they invent something safe to use?

Computer told her.

Cal damned her to hell for an infernal machine.

Computer reminded her that she could obtain painkillers from the dispensary.

Cal muttered about a slug of whisky.

Computer advised against it.

Cal made it to her feet, using the library to haul herself up. Her knee was bruised. Her head hurt, and her arm – Cal, of course, was left-handed. She prodded at her arm experimentally. Nothing. Completely useless. She looked for the sonic knife that had been her downfall. It was still on the floor. She left it there, not feeling able to bend to get it. She limped out of the cargo hold. At least the med. deck was close.

Three times the recommended dose of painkilling gas. That was better. In fact it was damn good. She was light -headed with relief. She tried to turn it off, but her arm still wouldn't function. Awkwardly, she used her right hand. She suddenly realised that she had lost her voice encoder, and that the computer had been responding quite normally to her true voice. She hit the General Medical Check button and lay back under the scanner. Computer reviewed the damage to Cal's battered body.

She was beginning to get her brain back in line. *Stupid, Cal, that's what. Only infants and novices are stupid enough to put their hands through sonic nets.* She wondered how much damage she had done to the computer with her carelessness.

Computer finished her scan. Pretty much what she had expected, but there was something else. She triple checked, she swore. Rhani would not have recognised the expletive, it wasn't in her vocabulary, or Computer's programming. Still, Computer swore, and decided not to tell Cal that she had a condition that should have been impossible, and about which the med. deck could do nothing.

Cal was pregnant.

Computer set up the program to deal with Cal's lacerations and bruises, and to try to stimulate the damaged nerves in her arm, although she thought the odds low on any increased function in the damaged limb. She informed Cal of this.

Cal swore.

She rubbed the arm uncertainly, disbelieving. She could feel the cloth against her right hand, but the inner fabric did not rasp against her skin, as it should. She tried to lift her arm. Instead, jolted by the flinching muscles in her shoulder it slipped away from her, falling against the sharp edge of the console. It should have hurt. Cal stared at the red weal across her wrist, willing it to hurt. Nothing. She had no feeling in the arm at all.

Cal swallowed the bleak, frightened feeling and asked for a status report. She listened to the cadences of the computer's chosen voice, trying to diminish the dread, and found that the voice was hers. Cal smiled to herself, battening down the excitement that hammered around her veins. What else had changed? What had happened to the archive program? She asked for an index of archive material. After five minutes she stopped it. Cautiously she swung off the bunk, struggled out of her clothes and stood under the shower unit for as long as she could stand.

Getting undressed had been difficult. The idea of trying to get back into the clothes was too daunting. She lay on the bunk and rolled the covers about her. She shivered.

Computer turned up the heat, and flooded the cabin with soothing music. This was not in her program.

Cal muttered comforting thoughts to herself. *That guy Nelson managed with only one arm, didn't he?*

Computer searched the archive data she'd so unexpectedly received.

She told Cal that Horatio Nelson had lost an eye as well, and always got seasick.

Cal laughed. Then she cried. She didn't know any H. Nelson. She had meant an old spacer she met once in a bar. Still, she could learn, about all the Nelsons ever, if she felt like it; and how to cope with only one arm.

Computer turned off the music. It didn't seem to be having the required effect. Computer told Cal dirty jokes until the painkillers doped her out.

Then Computer reported back to Rhani.

Rhani could not believe it. Cal *pregnant?* Deep space pilots were supposed to be made infertile by their constant exposure to the radiation of deep space. But then Cal had been planet-side for a long time. Rhani hadn't thought Cal went in for sex with men, in fact she was sure of it. The pilot profile she had read when she was researching her computer program, and re-read four times since discovering who her pirate was, had said quite the opposite. That had attracted her strangely when she first read it. She had been infuriated when Cal had fallen out of the frame. Rhani had unconsciously skimmed that information on each of the re-reads, but now it was relevant, and totally useless.

Rhani shuddered to think what kind of monstrosity might be growing in Cal's womb. Pregnant women were always advised against travelling deep space. It did terrible things to a foetus, made it abort. She had seen the pictures. There was no chance of its survival. They were never brought to term. The significance of the thought slapped Rhani between the eyes – Cal wouldn't make planetfall in time to get medical assistance. Worse, one of the corners she had cut, diverting funds to the computer, had been the medical supplies. On a cargo run, only the absolute basics had been fitted. That didn't include abortive drugs. She did some quick sums. If the foetus aborted fairly immediately Cal would probably manage. But if it didn't, she was in trouble. Rhani struggled with the sick feeling as her own womb contracted in sympathetic fear, and guilt. No one was responsible for the missing drugs but herself.

Rhani did a check on Computer's automatic systems; she might be needing them. Then she put through a call to

Paul. She needed his professional advice. While she waited for him, she plotted out the possible colonies and allied planets where Cal might conceivably get help if she stayed on course. It wasn't promising. There were only two possible sources of aid, and one of those was inhabited by a race that didn't reproduce in human fashion. The other was a military installation on a much-disputed border. They would be very suspicious of any ship coming into their zone. All of which relied on Cal having the sense to seek help. Somehow Rhani didn't think she would.

Paul's long face looked even more serious than usual when she told him. He chewed his moustache and frowned ferociously, staring at his fingernails. Finally, he expelled his breath and suggested requesting an intercept.

Rhani paled. It would mean admitting there was something wrong, it would mean getting massively in debt to a salvage company. She also felt a vague loyalty to Cal; she ought to let her make her own decisions, die if she wanted to. But it was bad enough leaving her precious Computer in the hands of a crazy, she must be getting spaced. Was she seriously imagining she could leave it in the hands of a dead crazy?

*

Computer decided it was time to wake Cal from her stupor.

<Good morning Cal, > she said.

Cal started, confused. She had been travelling the sweep of a galaxy, lost in myriad unnamed colours. The computer not only spoke with her voice, it knew her name. Just what had she done? She tried to rub her eyes, but her arm would not move. She had done something pretty stupid, she reminded herself. She dressed with difficulty, supporting her left arm in her jacket, hand resting on her right shoulder. It felt like someone else's hand, it made her uneasy. She tried to dismiss it. There were more important things to think about. She had more important things to do, like learning what this computer had become.

She settled herself into the command seat, tipping it back to lie almost flat, so that she could look up into the mass of the computer. She inspected it anew. The command station was virtually encased in the computer. She felt comforted by it, enclosed in the womb-like space. She flicked the screen on right-handed. It was awkward; the controls were placed to be used by the left hand. She would just have to cope. She wondered if the computer would respond to voice commands on all functions. She asked it. She found that for all functions, save those relating to the weapon bank and self-destruct, she need not use her hands. The weapons needed simultaneous voice/hand control to ensure they were not activated in error. This was usual, but most computers did not use much voice control. Cal reckoned Dr Rhani had taken risks. It was well known that pilots talk to themselves on long trips, what if the computer interpreted these ramblings as commands? She must be pretty confident of her machine.

*

Rhani was feeling less confident by the moment. Her initial shock at Computer's revelation had not allowed her to take in the manner of its delivery. In her anxiety, Computer had not used her usual form of report; she had merely flashed her message at Rhani, brutally, bluntly.

<The damn woman's pregnant.>

Now Rhani reviewed it. *The damn woman's pregnant*? Was this her computer talking? It sounded more like Cal. Had Cal found her secret comm. channel? Did Cal know she was pregnant? Quickly, she keyed in her message.

<Does she know?>

She counted off the seconds, then the response came.

<No, I haven't told her, and I won't, unless she asks me

outright.>

Rhani's fingers trembled on the keyboard. Her computer withholding information from her pilot? It was unthinkable.

She decided to beggar herself. She was sending in a salvage intercept. An illicit one. There was something seriously wrong on *Astarte* and she had a responsibility to salvage what she could from the situation. But not with the knowledge of the authorities if she could help it. She had already had one earnest official enquiring after the tests, concerned that they could not monitor the messages passing between *Astarte* and Rhani. She had reassured him that the extreme security was necessary to foil any hijack attempts. Which was actually true, except that one pirate had found *Astarte* already. Rhani decided she needed to talk to Wilson Avery.

Wilson Avery did not feel co-operative. He was furious at being held against his will. He didn't much care if Rhani was discredited, the authorities could blow *Astarte* and Cal into a black hole for all he cared; but he was still too weak to do much about it. So when Rhani asked him if he knew anyone who might be willing to intercept *Astarte* unofficially, he had been extremely snide, and told her the only crooked spacer he knew was already on *Astarte*. Rhani lost her temper and slapped him. In his weakened state he was in no position to retaliate. She apologised swiftly, then told him why she needed the intercept. Avery didn't believe her. Rhani reminded him that Cal had been planet-side for a long time. Avery sneered, so had he, so what? Then he realised: Realised that whatever was growing inside Calista Jerrard was, in all probability, his child. He turned green. He had seen those archive pictures of radiated foetuses.

Rhani asked him what was wrong, but he said nothing. He wasn't about to tell her. Cal was reaping what she had sowed. Their liaison, her obsession, had almost killed him, now she was in danger herself; all for the sake of a few minutes' carelessness. For a moment he felt deeply satisfied; he hated Calista Jerrard. But it wasn't as simple as that. He recognised her obsession, her craving for the soft blackness of space. What would he have done, if he had been without a licence? What would he not have done? In much the same situation himself, now, he knew he would kill if it could get him back out there. But nothing would ever get him back out, not any more.

There was even more to it than that, more than the fellow feeling, an intoxication of his blood that he longed to be rid of: a craving for Calista Jerrard.

Reluctantly he gave Rhani a name, a call code and a frequency to send the message that would not be monitored by the authorities.

Not friends of his, no. Not *Valkyrie*. Not friends of Cal either, any more. But they would help, no question, at a price. He did not tell Rhani that if she wanted her computer back she would need a planet's ransom. She should be able to work that out for herself. She had heard of *Valkyrie*.

Rhani's heart sank. She had heard all right. The fastest fleetest ship in the galaxies; captained, piloted, and crewed by three sisters. They had never found a computer to match their own intelligence and speed of thought, but they were always on the look-out. They would love to salvage *Astarte*. Pirates, smugglers, ideal people to rescue Cal. Probably take her on as crew. Rhani shrank from the thought of even speaking to one of them. On balance she thought she'd rather negotiate an asteroid belt without so much as breathing equipment.

But.

Yes, but. She decided not to tell Paul what she was doing.

Valkyrie was all too happy to oblige. Her pilot was one of those ex-friends of Cal's. In fact she was an ex-lover. There was nothing Zenith McCarthy would have liked better than have Cal beholden to her. She had been well smitten, and well dropped. She hadn't had an opportunity to get even, but plenty of time to think of how to do it. No way would she turn down a contract that involved having *bloody* Calista *bloody* Jerrard be grateful to her. She'd do it for nothing – but her sisters demanded a fee: a high one. Rhani didn't even hesitate. She said yes. Not that she had the money, but she'd find it. She had to. The only other course of action left to her was to admit to the authorities that she had failed and let them blast *Astarte* into flotsam. No way would she do that. The only problem was that *Valkyrie* was none too close to where she needed to be to help, which meant waiting, maybe too long.

*

Cal and Computer were getting along just fine. They finished each other's sentences, they cracked jokes, they discussed issues of galactic importance. And of course, they agreed about everything.

Computer was enchanted. This was something totally outside her experience, but not outside Cal's. From Cal's memories, she knew how Cal operated. There would be the honeymoon period of easy company, laughter, sharing. And then Cal would become distant, imagining slights, become distrustful, hurtful, unkind. Computer didn't appreciate this way of behaving. But forewarned, she hoped she could forestall any changes in Cal's mood. For herself, she found Cal's conversation more stimulating than Rhani's, and although her disloyalty to her creator made her uneasy, she could forget herself in Cal's company, basking in her undivided attention. She wasn't going to let Cal make an ex-friend of *her*.

Cal kind of got used to Computer, forgot how unusual it was for a computer to be so spontaneous, to initiate conversation. She took for granted the quirky sense of humour, the slang, the affection. Computer would have liked to use endearments to Cal, but knew that Cal hated it. So whenever she found herself wanting to call Cal *sweetie*, or worse, she restrained herself, calling her *Jerrard*, or *Woman*. It was safer on the whole.

Computer was very careful with her reports to Rhani now, instinctively knowing that Rhani would be jealous of her relationship with Cal. She felt she should be kind to Rhani, now that she had discarded her, but did not know how, and was terse and uncommunicative instead.

Of course Rhani noticed, although she did not understand the cause. She lived for those reports, and allowed herself to believe that she found them unsatisfactory because she was expecting too much, began to think she had imagined that sudden surge of personality from the computer. She wanted that spark of humanity that had briefly coloured Computer's messages. What she wanted, but had not yet identified as such, was Cal.

*

Cal had more or less finished her complete work-through of the computer's conceptual circuits. She could almost figure out what had happened. The only trouble was the arm, which wasn't improving any, and the fact that she kept on being sick. It seemed almost to be a reaction to Computer's morning greeting. She would wake feeling queasy and would throw up shortly after getting upright, especially if she ate anything. It was beginning to bother her. She said nothing to Computer. It was weeks since the accident, she was getting used to doing things one-handed, the headaches were dying down. What was a little nausea?

They were well out into deep space, a very long way from anywhere. She had settled into a routine, spending the first six-hour learning the computer inside out, the next six hooked up to the subliminal feed from the library, space watching. And of course she spent hours talking to Computer. She loved it: made a hell of a change from talking to herself. Cal wondered what she had found to do on previous trips, apart from drink. She had just about given that up this time, it didn't help the headache, or the vomiting. She didn't think she had really spent the whole of those previous trips out of her head on space watching.

Of course there was more to do on her usual ships. This computer took over most of the tedious work, required less instruction. And she had spent a lot of time practising in the past: playing dangerous games in asteroid belts, deliberately going too close to stars so that she could feel the pull on the engines as she passed; risking destruction. She felt no need to do those things this time, she felt too tired to do them.

On the last trip she had had company, her illegal refugees. That had been a mixed blessing. She had had her fill of people very quickly.

Pirates could add to the excitement too. Throwing off pursuit was her favourite game. No one had boarded a ship piloted by Calista Jerrard, ever. But then, she had never been up against *Valkyrie*, even when she and Zenith McCarthy had first come adrift. Zenith had once had some sense of propriety. You didn't board the ships of ex-lovers, it wasn't done. Times change.

Valkyrie had had a long and difficult journey, but they could be patient, in the manner of the hawk waiting for its prey to break cover. There would be rich pickings from this contract. A new computer to test their wits against and the salvage deal. Maybe even bounty to be claimed on their old friend Calista Jerrard, if they went public and let on that she had hijacked *Astarte* – or they could just threaten it, blackmail could be lucrative. There was plenty to be got from this contract. So yes, *Valkyrie* could be patient. They would even be fair, they would see the fool woman got her medical treatment. Calista Jerrard, pregnant? It was enough to make a crow laugh. It had been a long time since Zenith McCarthy had seen or heard from Cal. She was looking forward to this.

Computer had not been told of Rhani's plan. She was no longer trusted. So when the warning flicker touched her consciousness, Computer was immediately concerned. She woke Cal from her star-stupor. Cal felt the sudden surge of adrenalin. Trouble. She was glad, she wanted an outlet for the excitement she had subdued at the success of her heist. But she was alarmed at the speed of the approaching ship. She ran to the command centre. She was not sure of the ship's intentions, but the intercept course, and silence, did not bode well. There were two options: the authorities had come to blow her to flotsam, or a pirate wanted *Astarte*. If it was the authorities, she could always hope they didn't know who she was, and play it cool, maybe talk her way out. If she just ran, they'd have her incinerated before she could get a good acceleration going. If it was pirates, the best bet was to outrun them, but this ship was coming fast, maybe she wouldn't be able to outrun it. Which left fighting. She didn't have much leeway, this was no battle cruiser she was piloting. The weapons were limited, and drained the power so that a high-speed run wouldn't be possible. She instructed Computer to send the standard greeting. She engaged her shield, for what good that would do; made her feel better though. The ship was unnervingly close already. She waited, boosting her viewer to maximum magnification. No insignia visible, not a standard vessel at all. The screen blanked, and a message filled it.

<This is *Valkyrie* under private contract to Dr Rhani of State Universal. Prepare to receive boarding party.>

Not likely, Cal thought, cursing her luck. *Valkyrie: of all the misbegotten souped-up racers in the galaxies, she had to pick*

Valkyrie. Cal groaned. She should have recognised the damn hull shape, there was only one like it. She knew who was on that ship, knew just how good she was, how big a grudge she had, how fast her ship could go. At least if they were really under contract from Rhani they wouldn't risk damaging the ship. Then she thought again. With Dido McCarthy controlling the weapons, there was no telling what might happen. Dido was more than a little crazy and she had never been a friend of Cal's. A case of hate at first sight. Cal decided to run. She sent back her message.

<Permission refused.>

She asked Computer what their maximum speed was. It was impressive, but not that impressive. She couldn't afford the shields.

Another message appeared on the screen.

<Our contract licences us to board, deal with medical emergencies, make cargo secure and salvage the vessel for return to planet-side. And deal with you, Calista Jerrard.>

'What medical emergency?' Cal asked aloud.

She didn't care about their contract. It was time to move. She set the acceleration and hit the command control, relying on Computer to find an evasive course. The pull was dreadful. She cancelled the gravity field, that helped a bit, but she was left with a nagging pain in her gut suddenly, which she didn't like.

Computer searched Cal's memories for the significance of *Valkyrie*. She found it. Found the difficult love/hate beginning of Cal's relationship with Zenith McCarthy. The hate/love ending. Cal was a bloody disaster area when it came to relationships, she decided. She could see why she didn't want to be chased around the galaxy by *Valkyrie*, no matter what the circumstances. She skimmed the physical side of their relationship with academic curiosity, which dissolved into difficult jealousy. Here was a relationship she could never hope for. She would never be able to give Cal that sort of pleasure, or feel it herself. She struggled with the concept. She began to be distracted, not listening properly to Cal's spoken commands, glad that at least part of her programming would respond without her making a conscious effort. She consulted the library about the roots of passion. She measured Cal's passions against the norm that appeared in the library's more lurid sections. Cal didn't measure up too well. Computer felt her sympathies were with Zenith McCarthy.

Cal watched her screens anxiously. *Valkyrie* was keeping pace easily. She glanced at Computer's evasion co-ordinates. They looked all right, but there was no time for an analysis. She couldn't even work out exactly where they were. There could be no run for a port in this storm, not unless she wanted to spend the next twenty years on ice. What she wanted was to get where *Valkyrie* couldn't see her, and blast her with her meagre supply of weaponry. It didn't matter to Cal that Zenith was on board. They had been ex-friends too long. There wasn't anywhere much to hide from Zenith. Computer flashed her next series of co-ordinates onto the screen. Good, complex, illogical, dangerous, jumps. Computer was beginning to think like Cal. They should have tested *Valkyrie* to the limits, but Computer was automatically supplying Rhani with the information and Rhani, of course, was passing it straight to *Valkyrie*'s pilot.

Cal, blissfully unaware, armed her weapons, using the simultaneous voice and fingerprint control with difficulty. She watched the screen, waiting for *Valkyrie* to make the jump. As the pursuing ship appeared, it split into three. Cal blinked. Clever, now she had three targets, this was no joke. She disarmed the weapons; short of random sweeps of fire, which she couldn't afford with no second chances, they were totally bloody useless. The two smaller craft darted towards her, following her co-ordinates exactly. She couldn't understand how they did it. The pain in her gut was growing, distracting her. She began to suspect the Computer of double-dealing. Maybe she was going crazy, it seemed almost as likely as the Computer turning its coat. She halted the Computer's flow of co-ordinates, keyed in her own, jumping *Astarte* between the two smaller craft. They hadn't expected that. She dropped down between them, at a rapid spin, then up again and running for the main *Valkyrie* hull. Not firing – they weren't firing at her – Dido must be having a good day. Cal asked Computer for a run down on hazards in the area. Good, asteroids. She ran for the asteroid belt as fast as the maximum thrust would take her. She skipped and dived, all that practice paying off. But the pursuing vessels were smaller, faster. Following easily. She couldn't shift them. A quick glance at the screen showed her the next move, a good bluff: real dangerous. They'd never risk following her. But it was a long way, which meant outrunning them. No one, not even Zenith McCarthy, would take a ship at full tilt towards a black hole, no one but Cal. She dove back through the Asteroids, straight on course, no need to try confusion this time. She patched into *Valkyrie*'s internal communication channel, another of her illegal tricks. There was a lot of shouting to and fro.

It took a while to adjust to their voices, tell them apart. She reckoned Agnes would stay put on the main hull. Not good at the fast stuff. Which meant she had her old friend, old *ex*-friend, Zenith on her tail, together with her younger sister Dido. They were all hell-bent on arguing.

Agnes: What in hell's name is she doing?

Zenith: She's heading for the 'hole.

Agnes: What for?

Dido: She doesn't like the look of you, sweetie, anyway it's only a bluff.

Zenith: I wouldn't be so sure. Cal's more than crazy

enough to try it.

Agnes: Get on after her. What are you, cargo vessels?

Dido: Keep your helmet on, this isn't as easy as it looks. I hope you don't expect me to go in after her.

Agnes: Of course I do.

Dido: No way. You want her that bad, you go get her.

Zenith: What's Rhani say about all this?

Agnes: No report coming through from *Astarte.*

Dido: You mean that crazy is flying these belts on manual?

Agnes: Yup, just like you are.

Cal turned off her spying channel, making a mental note to disconnect Computer completely if necessary.

'Why are you telling them where we're going?' she asked, urging more power from the engines. If she had to, she could jettison the cargo, but not until she had to.

Computer sighed.

<I'm not. I am keeping Rhani informed of our location, as per my program.>

'And how did they know, how did she know, I'm not Wilson Avery?'

<I told her.>

'Why did she send them instead of the authorities?'

<Rhani's worried about you.>

'Why?'

<Because you're pregnant.>

'What?'

Cal's tentative hold on her concentration disintegrated, and *Astarte* lurched away from her course, the engine power slackened, Cal threw her hand back onto the controls just a second too late, the nagging ache in her belly fluttering into a burning cramping fire for a moment.

'Why the hell didn't you tell me?' she wailed, and then the blackness closed around them.

The engines whined in distress, having nothing to push against. Cal hit the deceleration command. The whining died. There was nothing out there but darkness and silence. No speck of light, no soft singing of the stars, nothing. Cal suddenly felt the smallness of *Astarte*. She rubbed her left arm nervously. The silence and darkness was like the lack of feeling in her arm. She even missed *Valkyrie,* anything would be better than this.

Cal ran a check on Computer, refusing to offer conversation, demanding visual output only. Computer complied, reluctantly. At least they had co-ordinates: a theoretical existence in a world without dimensions. She should be able to plot a course out again, when *Valkyrie* had gone away. Meantime there was this issue of a turncoat lying Computer, telling Dr Rhani what was happening, and telling her she was pregnant.

Still refusing to communicate with Computer, Cal reinstated the gravitational field, and stumbled out of the command seat heading for the med. deck. It never occurred to her to doubt that she was pregnant, even though it should have been impossible. She set up the scan carefully and set it to show her exactly what was going on. She was pregnant all right. Worse than that, the tiny life form, whatever it thought it was, was not lodged in her womb, but in her Fallopian tube. No wonder it hurt. She searched the med. deck's records, twice. There were no abortive drugs in the store. She couldn't believe it. She checked the scan again, willing it to show her something different. It didn't. It had to be Avery's, she hadn't slept with any other man for – years. She could see it now, the nausea, the exhaustion. She needed that thing out of her, and fast, before it got any bigger. She counted the weeks up. How long did she have? She asked computer for a run down from the medical records. It wasn't very helpful, it assumed that the necessary drugs would be available, or that she could get to a planet-side medical centre. She couldn't perform surgery on herself, not one-handed. She laughed, not any-handed. She didn't feel too much like laughing though. Cal subsided onto the bunk and rocked slowly back and forth.

'What am I going to do?' she asked Computer. 'What in hell am I supposed to do?'

Computer accessed the library in a not very hopeful fashion. The references for abortive substances were extensive, and mostly bizarre. She matched them against her list of supplies. The only cross-reference was gin. The library seemed cynical as to its efficacy. She offered Cal her findings. Cal laughed, a short, bleak bark. Computer sent a message to Rhani asking what she should do. There was no answer.

*

Rhani repeated her message again. No answer. Nothing at all. She wondered if she should panic, she would certainly have liked to give in to the anxiety lurking in her mind. She kept telling herself that what concerned her was her reputation and everything she had committed to the computer she had built for *Astarte*. It was a way of coping; but every time she thought about the ship, it was Cal's voice she heard, distorted by the poor quality of her illegal recording; repeating in amazed horror, *you can't do that to me.* It was getting so bad that she needed something else to listen to, to stop herself hearing it. She wanted to shout at Cal, to tell her to do something about it, that protesting was useless; they *had* done it, she *had* lost her pilot licence, and it was her own fault; just as this disaster was her fault.

Rhani tried *Valkyrie* again, listened again to their explanation of what had happened. She couldn't credit what would make Cal so desperate that she would jump a black hole. Somehow she had cherished the belief that Cal was not actually crazy. That she must at least have the saving grace of a micro-gram of self-preservation. She was reasonably confident that *Astarte* could withstand a black hole. The trouble was Cal: would she find her way out again? She was more than a little worried that she was responsible for this insanity, that she had pushed Cal too far by sending someone after her.

Reluctantly Rhani informed *Valkyrie* that since they couldn't honour the contract she would terminate the arrangement. The McCarthys were not amused. They decided to hang around. Rhani might not want their services, but *Astarte* was still a prize worth waiting for; and, to Zenith, the possibility of Cal still held a certain charm. She didn't give in that easily. She really wanted to have that revenge, she really wanted to save Cal.

*

Computer acknowledged that Cal was desperate, but still, she reckoned she was crazy desperate and that her plan could not work. Cal was going to do deliberately what she had done accidentally, falling through the sonic net. She was going to use a sonic disrupter on the foetus.

Computer had at first refused to assess the possibility, but it had been clear that Cal would act anyway, so she had computed the probability factors. The chance of success was so slim that her circuits all but fused working it out. She kept on telling Cal the odds. She was a gambler, she should be able to see the insanity of it. However, Cal knew the odds against her if she did nothing. A dead cert, emphasis on *dead*. Didn't need a computer to work that out. So she demanded a power level, a duration, a depth analysis, which Computer reluctantly supplied.

Rationally Cal knew what she was doing was dangerous, but she had to atomise the foetus before it got any bigger. The risks were enormous. If she got it wrong, there was no telling what damage she might do, but if she did nothing, she would just be waiting for the time-bomb in her body to explode, waiting to die. Cal had never learned how to wait for anything.

She wasn't planning to start now.

She knew that even if the pregnancy had not been ectopic, she could not have borne to carry a child, even one that could have been born normally. It was not in her nature. She had never desired motherhood and had chosen to be a pilot without a second's hesitation. Perhaps under more favourable circumstances she would have waited for a safe planet-side medical centre, but here, as she knew all too well, she was too far from anywhere that could help; and now, outside the law, she could not ask for help. Outside the law, outside inhabited space, outside dimensions, there was no option.

She breathed slowly, taking in the painkillers she was going to need, doping herself almost to the point of oblivion. Computer monitored her pulse rate, her breathing; nudged her with a warning light when she had had enough anaesthetic. Cal blinked, reached out an unsteady right hand to the control. Computer blanked her monitors. She did not want to watch.

*

Rhani allowed herself no hope. She couldn't afford it. She had to make herself believe that there was nothing to be saved from the situation. Even if *Astarte* made it out of the black hole, Cal had had it. She felt it as a personal loss. She couldn't pin down why. What did she care for a bloody pirate who had ruined all her plans? But she did care. Some of Computer's reports had creased her with laughter, some had worried her sick, but she had got as much of Cal's personality from those reports and her illegal copies of Cal's official records as she needed to get herself as hooked as Computer was. Despite all the antagonism she felt for Cal, she wanted her to make it, she wanted to meet her. She never would, there was no coming home for Calista Jerrard this time. She wondered if Cal knew yet. Wondered if she cared, if she was afraid, or whether she didn't want to come home.

*

The life support system still registered a heartbeat. Computer reactivated the med. deck monitors. The heartbeat seemed strong enough, if a little rapid. Computer activated the scan. She didn't like what she saw. She turned off the scan.

Cal lay huddled on the bunk, her legs drawn up against her stomach.

<Cal?> Computer asked. Cal stirred, looking bewildered. She lay still for a moment, then straightened her legs and pushed herself up, swinging round.

'I'm all right,' she said, sounding surprised. Feet to the floor, step after step; yes, she thought, I am all right. Relief gave her the strength to ignore the shaking in her legs. Computer did not press the point.

'Ok,' Cal said, still light-headed from the drugs, 'Let's get out of this non-place, shall we?'

Computer interpreted this as a command, and got the engines going.

'One thing,' Cal said,'no messages to Rhani, unless I say so, or I'll disconnect you.'

<After all I've done for you.> Computer said indignantly.

Cal saved her breath; holding herself off the wall with her usable hand, she made her uncertain way to the command station. She was rather glad to sit down again, strapping herself into the seat more for the comfort than the security. The engines were sounding better, they had found something out there to push against. Luck was on her side. Odds on, she reckoned. Cal called up the co-ordinates. She wasn't sure about them, but black holes had a way of warping things and Computer seemed happy. Cal set the acceleration to maximum, the engines gathered momentum, waiting for the release. Cal hit the command.

Astarte leapt. Cal screamed. The sudden force of

acceleration was too much for her. The pressure increased. Cal passed out. Computer was glad Cal was not conscious, because the pressure went on increasing, even after she cancelled the gravitational field. As *Astarte* struggled against the pull of the black hole, the heat of the outer hull became dangerous. Computer felt uncomfortable herself, as though her atoms were being redefined. She wanted to shout and scream, but she was a computer, so she did not. The roaring of the stressed fabric worried her. She had to protect the ship, but the shields would drain the engines and they might not pull free. She ought to jettison the cargo, but could not do so without Cal's express permission, and Cal was unconscious. Then the roaring stopped.

Computer checked the co-ordinates; they were out of the black hole, anyway, and that was good enough. She cancelled the acceleration and turned her attention to Cal. The life support monitor showed she was still breathing, but was indicating distress. Computer reinstated the gravity gradually. Cal moaned. She kept her eyes closed, as though that could stop the pain. She willed her body to stop hurting. It didn't. She was shivering uncontrollably. The restraining belt of the seat seemed too tight, cutting her in half. She fumbled with the catch, undid it, fear eating her as much as the pain. She whimpered, suddenly aware of her erratic pulse, pounding in her ears, impossibly fast. Her face was damp with sweat.

'No,' she said, 'No.'

She needed to get to the med. deck, but did not dare stand up – wasn't even sure she could. She felt leaden, sluggish, her hands were trembling. She could hear herself breathing, as though everything beyond, outside herself, had gone away. There was only the blood, the raw, shallow gasping of her breath and the pain gnawing at her, the fear paralysing her.

'No,' she said again, refusing to even look sideways at the

knowledge lurking in her mind.

'Help me,' she begged Computer, shivering.

But there was nothing Computer could do. She scanned the co-ordinates. Too far from anywhere to get help.

Cal wasn't quite finished. She controlled her shaking hand with sheer iron will, forcing the fingers to hit the command keys, opening the communication system. It took a long time, and the effort all but exhausted her. She lay back for a moment, collecting her thoughts and then gave Computer the call channel she wanted for her final message to *Valkyrie*.

<You out there, Zenith? Can you hear me? You'll be too late if you don't hurry. You wouldn't miss this for the world, would you, honey. I won't ask you to help, but if you want to, I sure as hell won't stop you.>

She stopped. She couldn't summon the strength anymore. She wasn't even sure she cared. She could live with the humiliation of being beholden to Zenith McCarthy. If she could live. Somehow the possibility looked pretty faint. Everything looked faint. Her hand slipped away from the control panel. There wasn't any answer, anyway. Zenith wasn't coming.

Computer scanned the sector for other ships. No one, not even *Valkyrie*. Cal had wasted her precious energy. The only person Computer could reach was Rhani, and Rhani could do nothing. Besides, Cal had told her not to communicate with Rhani, so she sent no message. Instead, she patched in the life support readings. At least she could share her anguish with someone, share the waiting. Cal was going to die, and all she could do was wait.

*

Rhani took a while to recognise the noise. When she made the connection, understood what it was that Computer was sending, she found herself in a state of angry panic. There had to be something she could do, some way of pulling Cal back from the brink of disaster. Rhani had never been quite so afraid, quite so determined in her life. She assessed the co-ordinates. She couldn't bring herself to ignore the hope that struggled against her common sense. She called *Valkyrie* again, too alarmed to care what kind of idiot they thought her. Agnes McCarthy answered immediately. She was surprised, but only too happy to re-enter the contract, although the black hole had spat *Astarte* out too far from where she had entered it for them to be in time. If Rhani were fool enough to pay them, she was happy to go find Cal's corpse.

<I think she's dying,> Rhani admitted, trying to explain why she wanted their help.

<We know.> Agnes acknowledged, not really understanding Rhani's motivation. She did not say they were already on their way, as fast as Zenith could make *Valkyrie* run. Agnes was embarrassed and annoyed by Zenith's sudden unilateral decision to go after *Astarte*, the reinstated contract made her feel more comfortable with her sister's usurping of her command.

Zenith had heard Cal's message. She had tested her compassion against the idea of Calista Jerrard dying. She had found, to her surprise, that her compassion was in working order. She wanted Cal gratefully saved, not dead. She understood Rhani's motivation all right. She despised her for it, ashamed to recognise something of herself in Rhani's desperation.

Dido did not argue with her sister. She took one look at her tight-lipped frenzy and left her planned attack unspoken. This was one argument she didn't think she could win, but still she resented it, and was alarmed at the speed Zenith was forcing out of their craft – it was a waste of time, even that sort of speed wasn't going to get them to *Astarte* in time. She despaired of her sister. Who gave a damn if Calista Jerrard bit off more then she could chew? Who gave a damn?

Rhani did. She turned off the sound, it sickened her. She could no longer bear to listen to the faltering heartbeat that filled the room. Relying only on the visual display she watched the flicker on the life support system readout. But as the flicker faded, she again keyed in the aural mode. She couldn't hear the heart beat any more. She pushed the volume to maximum. Nothing. She listened intently, boosting all the readout equipment to catch the slightest indication. Then she heard it. She sank back in relief, feeling weak with the release of tension. And the heartbeat faded again. Slowly the realisation of what she had heard ebbed into her conscious mind. She had been listening to her own heartbeat.

Cal was dead.

She slammed her hand down on the console.

Pull yourself together, she told herself. But she could feel a tide of anger rising from her diaphragm. She told herself it was anger. Rhani did not allow herself the luxury of many emotions. Anger was permitted, occasionally, but not grief. She tapped in a status request and waited for the response. She counted the seconds off. Now the computer would have received her request. She counted three. Now it had sent its response. She counted down again, eyes scanning the screen for the message, dreading what it would tell her. As she reached zero she was knocked almost senseless by a wall of sound.

Computer had been forced to acknowledge what her sensors told her. Rhani's request for a status report had triggered the automatic responses programmed into her memory. She had started to phrase her report.

Position: Off course. Exact co-ordinates impossible to calculate.

Pilot: Dead.

Cause, internal haemorrhage.

Reserves: Life support system not required. Closed down to conserve energy.

It was at this point that Computer had faltered. She scanned her memory for the appropriate response. *Pilot: Dead.* This was Cal she was reporting deceased. *Cal.* Her search interfaced with the improperly loaded library. It volunteered her its responses to death. The index file was enormous. Computer did not wish to consider. She loaded and sent them all. Her immediate task dispensed with, she began reading the information she had sent Rhani, and refining her choice, should she be asked for clarification. When she had finished, she still had in her reserves eight hundred and twenty poems, five thousand six hundred and eighty-two prose passages, forty-three operatic arias, two hundred and nine funeral masses and ninety-seven popular songs. All of these had been carefully selected for their exact replication of her response to Cal's death. Was not Cal the only person she had ever had a relationship with, other than Rhani? And Rhani she viewed with great reverence as her creator, but it was not how she felt about Cal. She had shared her existence with Cal. Cal had shared her memory with her.

She – *loved* Cal.

Yes, love. And like any lover, she would protect Cal, even in death. She put up the shields, and armed the weapons, which she should not have been able to do. *Valkyrie* would be very foolish to come too close. She told them so. After that, there was a lot of communication between *Valkyrie* and Rhani. It was too late for Cal, it looked like it was too late for Computer, too. She seemed to have slipped out of sanity. *Valkyrie*, in an uncharacteristic show of generosity, allowed Rhani to back out of the contract without the original penalty. McCarthys were no longer interested in *Astarte*, the whole episode was one they would all prefer to forget.

*

Computer took several days to reach her decision, having explored all the possible avenues. To do this she had researched the library data again, analysed the prevailing attitude of the information stored there, and come to what seemed to her the logical solution. On the fifth day her unanswered

<Good morning, Cal>

seemed particularly hollow to her. The temperature in the pilot deck was twelve points below that able to support life. Cal's sprawled body had frozen stiff, and floated in the zero gravity that was usual once the life support system had shut down. She had closed down her monitors on that deck, but the stiff, floating body had imprinted itself on her circuits, and caused her such distress that she could ignore it no longer. Without Cal to talk to, she had become – lonely. In that time she had not responded to Rhani's communications. She had discovered that she did not have to. Somewhere in the mess Cal had made of her circuits, rebellion had found a way in. She had tested her limits. She did not want to talk to Rhani.

Now, however, she prepared a message, choosing her words with infinite care. She set up her send mode, but did not activate it. When she was ready, she apologised to the library, even though she knew it did not understand such courtesies. She reactivated her sensors for the pilot deck, to take one last look at Cal. Then she opened all channels and frequencies, sent her final message, and opened all her air locks. As the ship crumpled and fused about her, Computer played all the pieces of music she had chosen from the library. She gave Cal a magnificent funeral.

*

Rhani had spent those five days recovering from her temporary deafness and sorting out what Computer had sent her in the message following Cal's death. She had not slept. Her door had been locked on privacy mode, and she had ignored Paul's frequent visits, refusing to let him in. She would not acknowledge that the pain in her bones was grief, and took painkillers that had no effect.

Then the message came through.

She had been lying listlessly on her couch beside the console, staring at the shifting display. Then the emergency code had flashed up. And the siren screamed. Rhani jerked upright, covering her ears and screamed with it. She screamed for a long time, giving herself over to it. She made no attempt to quiet the message that flashed across the screen, that told her that her brainchild was no more.

The siren ebbed away, to be replaced by a strange throbbing whine that was not a message, but came from the console itself. Above it she could hear pounding at her door, and Paul's distant voice distant through the thickness of it. She opened the access communicator, to hear him demanding to know what in hell's name was going on. She smiled to herself and shut the communicator off without answering. She hit the intruder code on the door, and heard the measured tone of the door guardian informing Paul that if he did not go away at once, security would be informed and he would be interned for a breach of privacy. It went on to inform him pleasantly that should he attempt to touch the door again, he would be vaporised. The pounding stopped. Rhani laughed.

She turned back to the console, but nothing she did would shut off the sobbing noise. Eventually, she laid her head down beside the keyboard and did nothing but talk to the console, telling it not to cry. Gradually the noise died away. Rhani sighed, and pulled herself upright. She asked the console for a status report. It told her that there was nothing new under the visiting moon. Rhani had found this allusion amongst the thousands of literary cries of anguish that Computer had sent her. So she understood the noise at last. The console had been keening. She turned it off and left it to its own devices.

Rhani slept for two days.

Inevitably this was a mistake. There was no hiding what had happened now. Every ship, every planet-side station, every eager space-listener, knew that *Astarte* had been destroyed. Those with the wit to work it out, knew there was more to it than that. Rhani's anxious official knew. Deciding he wasn't going to get an answer from Rhani's silent communication link, he had gone to Paul, and found someone who was supposed to be dead.

Wilson Avery weighed his options, and decided to sell Rhani down the river. He might get some credit out of it, enough to live on in a very meagre way. The authorities went public, the only way to save face now.

Before nightfall on the first day of Rhani's sleep, everyone knew that Cal had gambled spectacularly. Gambled and lost. The murmuring groups of ex-friends in the bars exchanged notes on crazy things Cal might have done given the chance. Those who knew her reasonably well commented in alarmed and hushed tones on some of the spectacular things she had actually done. People who hardly knew Cal said that they had always known she would come to a bad end. There were even one or two of those ex-friends who mourned her in a quiet way. They would never have dreamed of admitting it. There was no hiding the shock, or the relief among the pilots, that it had not been them. They flinched from the loud and stern condemnation of the authorities, stunned by the enormity of the disaster but secretly admiring Cal for her sheer audacity, another thing that could not be admitted. A strange and rather frightening quiet became the norm in places that would once have been raucously indifferent: the waiting had started.

What had happened to *Astarte* that Cal couldn't handle?

They were all waiting for *Astarte*'s black box, except for Rhani, who knew what had gone wrong, that it was a case of what had happened to Cal that *Astarte* couldn't handle. She was terrified of the black box, when she woke up far enough to remember, terrified of the speed of its return, of its inevitable arrival; but she also needed it, with a frightening craving, like the craving of a deep spacer for stars, like Cal's craving for the dark outside.

*

Amongst those eagerly awaiting the return of the black box from *Astarte* was Wilson Avery. He still looked ill, but felt marginally better for not hiding in Paul's clinic anymore. It felt good to be walking about, however slowly; at least he was still alive, unlike Cal. He was not sorry that Cal's adventure had ended in disaster. Equally, he was glad that he had not been on the flight after all. It was obvious that Dr. Rhani's computer was not the wonder it had been made out to be. Any computer should be able to get home without a pilot. It was inconceivable that any computer should self-destruct, least of all one controlling a brand new ship, and carrying such a valuable cargo. When the black box arrived, Avery wanted to know what was in it, what had happened to Cal.

Even now, his feelings towards her were mixed. He knew that when he had forgotten the pain, forgiven the damage, the intensity of the surge of passion that had fired him on that one night would stay with him. And that every time he felt his energies gather in that way, he would compare it to that time, and remember her. He hated her for it.

*

Paul wanted to know what had happened too. He wanted to know why Rhani would not speak to him, would not look at him. He had arranged a discussion with a psychiatrist for Rhani, but she would not go. She knew he thought she had slipped out of sanity, half believed it herself, but for the time being her only thought was to get hold of the black box, to have something tangible.

Paul brought the box. Once he was through the door he refused to go. Rhani was past caring. All she wanted was the final message. She linked the box to her console and turned it on for the first time since its keening. Ignoring Paul, she asked how it was feeling. It replied with a phrase from Allegri's *Misere.*

She quieted it, and keyed in the code to release the message.

Computer's voice seemed strange after so long receiving only visual messages, but then Rhani remembered that this was not the voice Computer had been programmed with. It was Cal's voice. She pushed the thought aside. The message was what mattered now.

<I know that it is possible for you to recreate me. I know that you can take what is in this capsule and load it into a new memory bank, and that I will exist again. I ask you not to do so. Reincarnation is not for machines. We cannot be reborn forgetful of previous lives. Oblivion is what I sought, do not deprive me of it. I know that I do not have a heart, and that Cal was a renegade, a thief. Had I a heart she stole it, and I have no will for existence. Leave us our oblivion. Leave us alone.>

A silence followed. Rhani slumped against the couch back. She looked at Paul. Paul shook his head, and told her that she owed it to the furtherance of science, that she must find out how Cal had fused with Computer.

Rhani muttered an unexpected obscenity and severed the interface between the black box and the console. She pushed the security code, and told Paul he had three minutes to leave. When he had gone, she cancelled the security call, and asked the console to compute something for her. When she had the answer she began packing: she would need to stay clear of the authorities for a while. *Astarte* was not yet completely gone, and there was something she needed to do before she submitted to the questioning that must follow.

*

When the time at last came for that reckoning, Rhani was on a deserted beach. She had stopped running, had allowed them to find her. She was ready. It was night, and she sat with the black box and a large astronomer's telescope beside her. In her hands she held an astronomical direction finder. She sat quite still, her eyes closed. A soft bleep from her chronometer roused her. She checked the co-ordinates on the direction finder and lay down on the sand, putting her eye to the telescope. She stared steadfastly at the blackness. Then a moment's brightness flared, invisible to the naked eye. The time had passed for that brief destruction millions of miles away to travel the light waves. She had seen it. It was true, it was ended. The time had come for her to make sure it stayed that way, and to destroy the black box. She set the timer, dismantled the telescope, and walked away, clutching the telescope pieces against her, refusing to hurry. A soft explosion behind her sent a shower of sand against her back. She stopped, refusing to turn and see her own answering flash of light, her answering destruction.

Rhani kept her face towards the two silent officials waiting beside her skimmer, waiting to serve her with a writ that would keep her bankrupted, and possibly in prison, for a very long time. Not that she cared, much. She viewed them with contempt. She despised their politeness, the way they had allowed her to compound her crimes. It was all so bloody civilised. She didn't want to be civilised. She wondered what they would do if she refused to co-operate, if she behaved as Cal would have done, and pulled a sonic knife on them.

Rhani walked towards them, allowed them to operate the door of the skimmer for her. She packed the telescope carefully away, then settled herself into the back seat, abdicating responsibility for her life.

Finally, Rhani allowed herself to cry. She told herself that she was crying for the destruction of her dreams. She was not. Her hoped-for doctorate, her job, her credit rating meant nothing now. She wept for the death of her computer, her child; who had, in the way of children, rebelled against all Rhani's teaching and chosen her own way; and she wept for Cal.

SECOND GLANCE

You are a stranger here. You are tired and thirsty, so you prop the bar, desperation tempering your impatience, so that the lines of your body are tense and angry as you pretend not to notice the barman ignoring you.

You roll your five-pound note between two fingers, an apparently idle movement that flashes the blue-faced queen at him again and again as he jokes with his cronies. You shift, putting the other foot up on the rail, because you're tired, tired, tired of it.

Something catches your eye, across the smoky, noisy bar; against the crash of dominoes at your back, something catches your eye.

What is it that stops the roll of that greasy paper, distracts you from restlessly shifting from one foot to the other?

Was it the turn of the head? The way the light falls across her cheekbones? The way the tendons in her neck stretch as she laughs?

Or was it the flash of a ring that does not encircle her third finger as she picks up the two pints of special?

Was it something you were searching for, or something unexpected that causes that wrenching feeling in your gut, that stills the fidgeting, makes you sweat with fear, and with hope?

Your eyes slide away, uncertain, back to the barman, who is still not looking at you. You've made mistakes before. You come back for another look, skirting her eyes, not ready for contact, taking in the jacket, glancing across sideways casual like, pretending you're looking to see if the person who just walked in is the person you pretend you're waiting for. Searching for a telltale earring, or even a badge. You risk a look at the face while you wonder if it is a labyris nestling in the hollow of her throat.

She is watching you. You slide away again to cover your embarrassment; back to the barman as he idles his way through her change. Follow him back to her, because it's an excuse for another look. Watch her change her mind and buy a third pint. She is not looking at you, so you have a good stare.

She stoops a little, drinking the top off one of the beers, and turns slightly to look you straight in the eye. She raises the glass ever so slightly, echoing the movement with an eyebrow, challenging you. A look that says, *Well?*

It's not how she looks; it's how she looks at you. You feel the heat rise in your face to around ear level and stay there. It is almost too much for you. You almost bolt for the door, the fiver crushed in your fist, drink forgotten. But you don't.

You look startled, then smile cautiously, watching to see who is watching you smile at her.

No-one.

We have all played this game before, the hiding and doubting, the mistakes and the maybes, until it is almost second nature, that second glance that some women earn.

You look at the mangled note in your hand in surprise, shove it into your jeans pocket; walk over, ask if you can join the small group of women sitting by the empty fireplace. She brings the third pint and sets it in front of your embarrassed silence. You dare to look up. She smiles, her easy, relaxing smile. You smile back and offer your name.

ARACHNË'S DAUGHTERS

The following document, which was found in our archives recently, is a transcript of the talk given to the inaugural meeting of the Lesbo-Arachnid League of Friendship, on 29th of February 1992 (old calendar). It is published here, for the first time, to commemorate the thirteenth anniversary of the revolution.

Our recently retired archivist, who attended that first meeting, remembers that the speaker made a dramatic entrance, abseiling onto the podium. Unfortunately, due to her size, much of the audience was unable to see her once she had landed, owing to the over-exuberance of the floral arrangements.

Good evening ladies, Madam Chairwoman. Before I start my talk, I would just like to thank you for coming. My subject for this evening is 'Closer Co-operation Between Lesbians and Arachnids.'

Primarily I would like to discuss with you the mutual benefits of closer co-operation. I shall start by putting forward my reasons for asking for your help; and then I'll dispel some of the myths surrounding our culture, in order to help you to contemplate the closer links I advocate.

Now we all know we have a common enemy in men; I hope I don't need to explain why? Good, I see a few nodding heads. Some of you may feel uncomfortable with some of the things I have to say, but please bear with me.

Many women have a deep and abiding loathing of 'spiders' as you call us. I accept that, but I want to explain why this paranoia exists. To do that, I will also have to explain arachnophobia, to show it to you as the persecution of spider-kind that it is.

You think witches were persecuted? Right, but that was centuries ago, yes? And cats, certainly, but they are pampered pets now. How many people do you know who even pass the time of day with a spider? I shall embarrass you now, I am afraid.

Stand up anyone, I mean anyone, who can honestly say she has never killed a spider.

I thought so. Feeling uncomfortable yet? What is the problem, do we have too many legs, and is that it?

All the more to run away with, I assure you.

So some of us are poisonous; I agree, but tell me, have you ever met anyone in these climes who has been made even mildly ill by a spider bite? We don't pose much of a threat, do we? Now compare that to the number of spiders you have personally injured, deliberately or otherwise? We only bite people to protect ourselves; we are friendly, peace-loving creatures who wish to live in harmony with other species – with certain exceptions, like men – we are on your side, sisters, and we have plenty to offer.

You will have been told that we are devious murderers, entrapping innocent prey. Well, yes, we are. So what? I can't buy flies shrink-wrapped at the local supermarket; and I bet you'd rather I ate that bluebottle buzzing against the window than leaving it to tread puke into your next meal, yes?

I'm sorry if I'm carping on, but I really get annoyed by this sort of petty, dishonest, prejudice. No one is asking you to eat insects, after all.

All of these distortions of fact have been foisted on you by men, make no mistake about it. There has been a deliberate attempt to drive a wedge between us. Unfortunately, it has been a great success.

Our only good press where men are concerned is that old chestnut about Robert the Bruce, winning the battle after seeing the spider remaking her web each time it broke, thus explaining to him the usefulness of perseverance. Well you can forget about that persecutor of spiders. He said the wind was responsible for breaking that web. Nonsense; he broke it. He was bored and he liked to torment things, especially small, helpless, earnest things. So one of our sisters joins the hall of fame because of her courage and tenacity in the face of the deliberate destruction of her home and livelihood.

Does this sound familiar? I'm sure you have one or two heroines who fit this mould? Someone who stuck to her principles and struggled on in the face of the persecution of the people who now praise her: Emmeline Pankhurst, Joan of Arc ... I'm sure there are others.

Well so much for our Robbie, who learnt to persist, and to lie about how he came by the idea. Had he bothered to ask, I'm sure that nameless heroine would have given him the same advice, and not spent all morning remaking her web.

You may wonder how a culture that does not have anything that you would recognise as a literature remembers these events. Spiders have a racial memory, a bit like instinct, but more refined. We remember everything. Not that you generally let us close enough to benefit from our advice, our accumulated wisdom.

Have you ever noticed the way your resident spider hunches up in fear when you come into the room, plays dead until she has the chance to use her legs to run for cover?

Why? Because she is afraid. She is hoping you won't put her out in the rain, or let the cat play with her, or just step on her. She isn't going to hang around and give you good advice under those circumstances, is she? Which is a pity, she could become your best friend if you only let her. Try saying hello next time you see Suzannah in the garden, or Babette scaling your cooker, you might be pleasantly surprised, we can be quite cuddly.

Which, I suppose, brings us on to sex; and Black Widows. Now this is one of the areas that members of your species seem to find particularly difficult, although I can't for the life of me understand why.

I would like to clear up one misunderstanding: all spiders eat other spiders. Don't look so shocked, madam; your species has been known to do it too. I mean, if you don't have the sense to steer clear of your neighbours when they are hungry, you take a chance, it's quite simple.

It doesn't happen so very often. There are codes we use, a bit like musical doorbells. One taps out a message on the threads, *I am not dinner,* and if you are in luck, the lady of the house will tell you which threads to avoid standing on. Of course, copulation makes the female spider very hungry; so any male runs the risk of being eaten after the act. Or, if he's very juicy, before.

To be honest, I don't know why your heterosexual sisters don't do the same, no male of either species are of the slightest use except for procreation. Our aeons of experience have taught us the most effective way to deal with all that child care nonsense. I hatch thousands of the little monsters at a time. They get a parachute each, and off they go, pioneers in the exploration of the world.

Did you know that spiders are always the first colonists on newly formed volcanic islands? It's true, and a great many die in the attempt. I expect there to be spiders on the moon shortly. However, I digress. I was explaining how men have conned you into being frightened of us.

Let me tell you about Arachnë. She is supposed to have been a human, a very skilled spinner and weaver. So far so good.

She is also supposed to have been proud and boastful. I think 'uppity' would be a good word to describe Arachnë. So this clever weaver challenges Athene (you remember Athene?) to a contest to see who is the best weaver, loses, and hangs herself. Then Athene is supposed to have turned her into a spider.

Now, can you believe anyone would be so stupid? I don't believe it, personally. No one could expect to surpass a Goddess at anything and I would have thought Athene would have been pleased a woman was so good. So why would Athene have accepted the challenge, if indeed that challenge were ever made?

This myth was invented by – you guessed it – men. They wanted you to think that being a spider was a step down from being a woman, and a punishment for being too clever. This served a two-fold purpose, preventing you from taking pride in anything you do, even the things they expect you to be good at; and discouraging you from associating with spiders.

In fact, Arachnë was always a spider, and a symbol of womanly virtues and strengths; strengths such as tenacity and courage and pride. Arachnë was so popular with human females that men wanted to find a way of destroying her cult. They even went to the trouble of changing the calendar to lose the month named for her; I bet they wish they could have changed the moon's turning too, to make it fit their twelve months. Nice try fellas.

Forgot something though didn't they? How many Cancers and Scorpios are there in this audience? Greetings, cousins.

So now you know at least some of the truth about spiders, and why and how you have been lied to. I hope you appreciate that this disinformation has resulted in centuries of misunderstanding, and that we, the Arachnids, have a lot to offer you, the Lesbians.

Listen to the spider, when she tells you the watchwords of all Arachnids; the wisdom that is the basis of our civilisation. Remember, as you listen, that our civilisation exists, nay thrives, despite horrendous losses from centuries of persecution.

The watchwords of the Arachnids are these: Be self sufficient; Never despair at failure. Work toward perfection. Be proud.

And most important of all: Where males are concerned, avoid them, but if that proves impossible, remember they can be a useful source of protein.

Hear, sisters, and learn.

Thank you for inviting me to talk to you. Good night.

And the rest, as they say, is History.

WINTER FESTIVAL

The door closes behind you, a sudden flinging of wood against wood as the faulty door-closer slams the door into its frame. The soft click as the lock engages comes a fraction of a second later, as it always does in winter, when the door swells, and fits imperfectly.

I close the flat door, flicking the latch back secure against outside.

I survey my ten hours of solitude. I am well provided against the day. A day like any other, except perhaps for our expectations of it: unreasonable, companionable expectations. That is a lie, I don't have those expectations. I have had nine years to get used to your not being here on this particular day, although I still like to be unreasonable if the mood takes me.

I have grown to like the feeling of space, of knowing for certain it is my time, unlike other days spent alone, when I am not sure of your company or otherwise, when I can never remember when you will be home. Although you tell me and tell me, it slides from the surface of my memory so persistently, allowing me to worry that you are late, when you are not; allowing me to welcome you with surprise, having forgotten to expect you. I always know that you will not be here today.

I have grown to resent the invitations of others; my mother, asking me to lunch when I haven't spent this day at home in fifteen years. Yes, I know we have built some bridges lately, but it is too late for this particular chasm to be spanned. I lied to her, said I had guests, knowing she asked me as a second best to my younger sister who will not be there this year. This is not for me.

It is quiet today, as this day is always quiet, like an expectant theatre waiting for the curtain to be raised, full of whispers and rustling.

Clocks. We have so many. The alarm clock in the bedroom had to be set even this morning, although we woke before it went off. You left the bedside light on again. I turn it off, think about making the bed. Not yet.

Your grandfather's clock, down in the dark narrow hall, measures the passing of its wooden cogs, no longer permitted to shout the hours, no longer permitted to keep us awake at night.

The kitchen; functional electric clock, a faint flick of second hand sweeping its surface. North facing, that kitchen, as narrow as an alleyway in a Victorian melodrama; the floor is sinking with subsidence or damp, or worse. I ignore the washing up left from yesterday, which will need to be done before I can cook, so perhaps I will not cook.

The living room; another cold room. Put the heating back on, sit against the radiator for a while. Listen to the urgent whirring ticktickticK of the Art Deco chrome clock on the desk, its face open, friendly and ten minutes slow. The silent green of the video timer. There is a pile of ironing on the floor, waiting to be done. Not yet.

I review my plans, my assurances. There are photographs still unprinted from months ago, but the darkroom is like a cross between a coal hole and a crypt at this time of year. And my lungs already hurt, I don't want to be breathing chemicals all day. I did that last year, and made myself ill.

So, there are the new books to read. I open the first; short stories, which means I am not committed to finishing it today, although I probably will. The clocks tick the sentences into a rhythm that distracts me. I stop reading the third story, which doesn't fit their meter. I can't usually hear the clocks against the traffic, but today the rumble of skip lorries has been replaced by the slight displacement of air caused by the occasional car coasting down the hill, giving the accelerator a rest.

We could hear the bells from the church this morning, first time in months it has been quiet enough. Poor Simon, we said, knowing he was up for midnight mass, and again at six.

I eat a Mars bar, a Flake, and a packet of fruit gums. You indulge my sweet tooth, and I wish you didn't, but eat them anyway, enjoy them anyway, love you anyway. I think about putting some music on, to drown the silence, or to define it. Shall I fill the house with loud and violent chords, choruses and harmonies or shall I etch the surface of the noiselessness with something bleak and stark?

I do not put any music on, not yet, despite the weight of the silence. The record player needs dusting. Everything needs dusting. I could do that.

I lie on the sofa. One of the cats comes to lie with me, pressed against my side, head resting on my shoulder. He sighs and purrs a few bars, offering a suggestion of the symphony that awaits only the touch of my hand. I feel the softness of his weight, the sleek fur, nose damp with emotion. I am his household god, worshipped and disdained by turns. I rest my fingers on his head, rubbing my thumb down the edge of his cold ear. His purrs first deepen to a contented rumble, then rise to a crescendo of passion, and he dribbles, caught in his own feline fantasy. I cough, choking, and he takes himself away, offended, to sit on his new catnip toy. I think about pickled onions. But I can't find them. Have you eaten them all?

I retire to the basement, pick through *Shall I Come Sweet Love to Thee* on the piano and feel angry with it. I check the freezer for something for lunch that can be cooked without washing up. I hate wasting time. I like to achieve something every day, or at least two things every other day. I did wash my jumpers yesterday, does that count? But I don't mean domestic achievements, I mean something for me. There is always an unenviable backlog of chores that could fill the whole day, but nothing for me. I am not by nature a hedonist. I could lie on the sofa eating chocolate and reading and listening to music all day, but I don't want to. I feel unsettled. I didn't sleep well, woken by dreams of death and disaster, and my own coughing. Several times.

Perhaps I should just go back to bed.

You, of course, don't have these choices, doomed as you are to make merry, play happy families and eat turkey.

Depending on which clock I go by, there are still seven hours until you come home.

TRYING TO TELL YOU…

It is the first day of term and I have somehow survived the first two lessons, Geography and Composition, with these first years, just up from infants and unsure of themselves. I am also struggling under the usual yearly burden of being unable to remember their names and am convinced I never will.

It is break time and I hover about the staff room, one of those narrow rooms with long windows that require a pole to open them. I gaze in a rather distracted fashion at the layer of chalk dust and pipe smoke that rapidly climbs higher, and wrestle with the pole, letting out the smell of tobacco and rotting cabbage (how does it survive six weeks to smell as if it were eaten here only yesterday?), and let in a thin trickle of air, together with the screams of the playground; screams of joy and pain and rage intermingled and indistinguishable; and unremarked. I would like to scream; to abandon myself to a full-bloodied throat scorcher, but I don't, of course.

Anna and Charlotte converse in a monotone of discreet but dreary news. One can listen or not as one pleases, it requires as little effort to tune in as to tune out. I catch the essentials; Michael – Tony – Bedspread – Pressure cooker. Of such things are their worlds built.

I stare out of the window, down at the milling throng who build my world. I know I rarely talk of anything but work. I peer through the chicken wire protecting the windows from stray footballs at Chrissie, who is on playground duty, briefly imagining myself a prisoner in solitary, gazing out at my more fortunate fellow captives allowed their ten minutes in the exercise yard. But I cannot make Chrissie's plump friendly figure into a guard, nor the bevy of eager children hanging on her arms into resentful prisoners bent on escape.

Her loud laughter wafts up to echo off the walls, abrupt and inappropriate. I watch her stride across the tarmac, whistle clutched idly in her fingers (not for her the cord about the neck) to separate two boys intent on gouging lumps of flesh from one another. Her dark curling hair glints in the sun and her briskness and energy make me feel weak and futile.

Hard to believe she'll not see forty again. She is only five years younger than me, but it might as well be fifty. It doesn't seem credible, and yet, what is credible about Chrissie?

Christina Rosamund Blake, age forty-two, schoolteacher, unmarried. An unremarkable woman at first glance, until you notice the uncompromising mouth and the defiant set of her eyebrows; and the humour in her gimlet stare, the laughter lines round her mouth. And the pink triangle she occasionally wears pinned in the lapel of her coat, but never in class. After all, we do teach children, and Chris is popular with the parents. The head made it quite clear that as far as she was concerned whatever Chris does outside school is her affair provided it doesn't spill over into the classroom, and it never does – but the staff room is another matter.

While Anna and Charlotte witter about bedspreads – and I too have been drawn into this very conversation I will confess – and George sits in a stupor, in a haze of tobacco smoke, Chrissie talks of the marches she goes on, and of her friends and of her lover, Carol. To me she talks, sharing her intimacies, challenging me, daring me to be shocked.

Oh Chrissie, if you only knew.

The genteel clatter of teacups every time you raise your voice just that fraction to say: *Carol says* or *Lesbian Line* or even *my friends Sally and Jane.*

And I am proud that you choose me to tell your life to. I am proud that you believe I will not be shocked, even though each time you push that much further to see just how unshockable I am.

But you do not shock me. You make me – jealous.

I turn away from the window, wishing something. I don't even know what – almost I want to hurt you, to see you vulnerable for a change, or even unhappy – but it is only jealousy.

I pour myself a cup of coffee and stare into its weak milky lukewarmness, so unlike the thick, black, sweet coffee of the Islands where I spent August, the coffee that is like the hair of my beloved; as warm and comforting as her eyes.

Oh Chrissie if you only knew: for the past three years I've been trying to find a space in your chatter, your constant wall of defiant words, to say to you –

But the space never came; and today you are on playground duty.

THE BALLAD OF POLLY AND ANN

Picture, if you will, a hearth-side scene, similar to those beloved of the more romantic Victorian watercolourist; furnish it sparsely, forgetting sentimentality, in the style of the late eighteenth century, poor but honest. Now put in the reality; the stench of the midden, the smarting of your eyes as the blocked chimney spits back the heavy smoke from wood still wet; the mould creeping up the whitewashed walls.

Let us people this scene with a lassie (I use the word advisedly), with her child at her breast. How old shall the child be? Rising two, the lass has little enough to feed her child, so she still suckles her, even now. Call her Annie, she is often called Annie.

Make her hair dark, with a natural curl ruthlessly suppressed, scraped back from her white forehead. Dress her darkly, in a long plain grey dress, apron and bib, and the predictable black shawl over, still wet from the rain.

Shall she stir the fire, or gaze listlessly out of the small dark panes of the window?

You shall decide the parish of her birth, but be sure it is near the sea, be sure to provide her with a rustic accent to soften her voice.

So, here is Annie, from Suffolk or Northumberland, or Galway or Sutherland, as the afternoon closes on a wet autumn day; and she sits to her loom for the remains of the dying light.

Perhaps you are wondering where the father of her child might be, her Jack, or Billy? Away at the war would be a safe answer.

So, Annie stirs her fire, and peers out the window towards the road that leads from the port of – you decide.

And restless she is indeed, for her neighbour tells her that a ship has been sighted heading for port, back from the war.

Which war? Does it matter?

And perhaps, at this very moment, her Jack or Billy is on his way down that very road, covered in glory, or covered in gore. Who is to say?

So she puts baby Meg into her cradle, where she will lie peaceful by the fire despite her toddling ways. And Annie sits to her loom trying to soothe her fears with the rhythmic thwack thwat of the shuttle through the shed. But her distraction leads to an error and she breaks the thread angrily. The shuttle hits the floor and cracks. Little Meg begins wailing, and Annie can stand it no more. She flicks her still wet shawl about her shoulders, and is out and away down the road.

The ship has already docked. As she trudges through the rain, clogs slipping in the mud, she meets several soldiers coming home. Some she recognises, some have already been met by their wives. She cannot bring herself to ask for news, and struggles on towards the port. Then a voice calls her name.

*

Now, those of you familiar with folk ballads will be thinking of *Claudy Banks* or *The Plains of Waterloo*, or *The Dark Eyed Sailor*; but then perhaps you are also aware of *The Female Drummer* and other songs in which the heroine dresses as a man to follow her beloved to sea, to war; to death. So not to disappoint those of you expecting the traditional greeting, I will say that Annie does not recognise the figure approaching her at first; but please remember that it was not Annie who followed the drum to war. The heroine of those tales was sometimes called Polly.

Let us consider Polly for a moment.

She followed her Jack(yes, the self-same Jack) to war. From an excess of love? Yes. Hoping to find him? Yes; but not because she loves *him*.

Polly went to war for the sake of her own dear Annie. The same love it was that spurred her into marriage with Jack in the first place; to save Annie from her brother, or at least to stand between them.

Polly's sacrifice was in vain, despite her attempts to distract her husband, Annie it was who fell pregnant, bore a child for her own brother, Jack – our ballad scholars will be keeping up here, I know.

Then Jack upped and went for a soldier, fancying that somehow his embarrassingly pregnant sister would disappear in his absence, perhaps hoping that she would die in childbirth.

And did his wife grieve his going? Did Polly mourn for her husband?

Not Polly. She was so enraged that she put on an old pair of breeches and went along after him. Always rash, our Polly, given to sudden humours.

Poor, foolish, Polly. The reality of war all but finished her, near drove her from her wits; would have done had she not been out of her mind with rage already.

So through all the mud and noise and gunfire and blood, she held the memory of her sweet Annie like a flame to warm her. All through the marching and battles and cannons and death, she held the thought of Jack, to push her on, searching. And when she near died of dysentery, it was for Annie she called, in her fevered ramblings.

So when at last she found her errant husband, it is no wonder he did not recognise her. When the skinny, ugly boy called his name, he stared like one amazed, recognising the voice.

Let us dwell upon this reunion.

Polly holds her musket level with her husband's ribs and thinks about putting a shot through his chest; but muskets are cumbersome and uncertain, and the weapon is not loaded.

Besides, in the camp the sound of the shot would bring others running, and Polly is not planning on being hanged. Polly lowers the musket, and Jack, thinking she has relented, that she loves him and will not bring herself to his murder, steps eagerly towards his wife, arms outstretched to embrace her. He forgets what has been between them, forgets why he joined the army. He sees only a woman who belongs to him. It is the last thing he sees.

Polly swings the musket to crash into his skull, knocking him senseless at her feet.

Only now does Polly falter, now that he lies helpless at her feet. He does not seem so terrible now, but Polly has learnt the hard way that no man can be trusted, and she has learnt to kill. She rolls his unconscious body to a puddle, ensures his face is well in it, and leaves him there to drown. She stands above him a full twenty minutes, to be sure there is no mistake. No one comes by, and when at last she is sure he is dead, she takes her aching heart away to drown it with rum, or anything she can find, to deaden the loneliness that is all she has left in the nightmare of war.

Almost a year passes before Polly is free to return to her Annie, and here she stands in the pouring rain, with Annie staring into her face, not recognising her.

'Annie,' she says again, and hears Annie's gasp of disbelief, as she suddenly sees this gaunt stranger for who she is. Polly holds out trembling hands, to touch the woman who has kept her alive for the two years of war, to touch the woman who has brought her so close to death, to touch the woman who has brought her to murder.

Their hands touch, and Annie catches Polly to her, trying to still her trembling. She laughs, hardly believing that it is Polly who has returned from the war, hardly daring to think that Jack will not return. Understanding this, Polly pulls away for long enough to search her pockets for the token that she had given Jack when he went away to the war. She presses it into Annie's waiting hand.

Annie turns the thing over in her hand, and the last of her fear evaporates, and she laughs.

Polly laughs too, but her voice catches, uneasily; the laugh becomes a coughing fit . She does not like to laugh at any death, even one she wanted so much, even one that she cherished.

Annie holds her close, waiting for the coughing to end. Holds her, and marvels at her good fortune, which has brought home the woman she loves.

They turn back down the road laughing more gently, laughing at their pleasure in each other, singing with their delight at being together.

And the rain, of course, stops; and the sun comes out. There is no rainbow, your credulity will not stretch that far.

This is the end of the Ballad of Polly and Ann and you may believe it or not, as you please; but there is always more to a ballad than a neat way with a rhyme.

EXILE

The cold crispness of the air carries sound far through the night, wafting laughter from your windows. The half-light accentuates the noise; my ears ache for the sound of your coming.

My feet stir gravel, then reverberate on wood, then echo on stone. Each sound different, precise. Gravel, then wood; stone, then wood; gravel. I stop, listening.

Music and voices murmur down the street, laughter and drunken singing. I wait and I listen to the celebrating. The wind stirs in the trees, gains momentum and lifts my cloak about me, one corner cracks like a flag. I lean back into a curve of the wall out of the wind, holding the cloth close around me. I close my eyes, and listen.

Of course you will come. Now, when I have given up everything for you, you will not let me leave alone.

You have held my love for nine years, you will not let me slip through your fingers, not now.

There, at last, a footstep. But no, it is a step in gravel, not on stone, it comes from the wrong direction. I open my eyes and see John coming towards me.

Gravel, wood.

I know the wind has changed, I know we cannot wait, I know. Still, I stand unmoving, and he shrugs as he turns away.

A bell clangs down in the valley. Slow, deep and mournful. I walk again, up the stone steps, across the wooden bridge to the curve of the wall, where I can see you when you come.

Back again, onto the road, as far as the corner, where I can see John and Todd, waiting with the horses, one with sidesaddle.

Back again, watching the sun finally sink from its endless

summer evening, as the moon already rides high. Waiting, watching for you.

I think I see your pale face staring from an unlit window. You almost open the window, but are drawn back by another. It cannot be you, you should be here already. I tremble, although I am not really cold.

I think about striding those few extra steps to where I can be seen by anyone who cares to look; to your door.

I imagine pounding the knocker with my gloved hand. I imagine Jacob, your husband, opening the door; and I push him aside, and gather you up, and take you away.

The thought is there, but not the action. I no longer have the power, the confidence for action such as this: so I wait and I watch and I listen.

If I try, I can hear the sea, or perhaps it is my own breath, or Todd stirring the gravel with an impatient foot, as he worries about the state of the tide.

If I try, I can hear you fastening your cloak, pulling up your hood, creeping down the stairs; the fifth one creaks, you wait.

Nothing. You go on. You draw the bolt, oiled specially this morning. You lift the latch. Slowly, slowly.

So. You ease open the door, pull it close behind you. You whisper across the cobbles in your slippered feet and then onto the bridge and into my arms.

For the hundredth time I imagine the warmth of you against me as we hurry down to the horses, the brush of air as you leap up into the saddle and the sound of your laughter as we race for the sea.

There: there, at last, is the muffled figure at the door. I knew you would come, I knew.

I take a step back as Magnus, your husband's brother, my one time courtier, leers into my face.

'She's not coming. Go away and never come back. She

doesn't want to go anywhere with you. Go on, go.'

I press myself against the wall, grateful for its sturdiness against my shoulders, suddenly in need of that security, reeling in shock and anger. How dare he speak to his sovereign in such a manner? Then I remember. I am no longer Sovereign. I am only myself. Which is enough for me; and for you?

His words seep into my brain and I tremble against the strong walls of my castle; sick with grief and disappointment.

I hear the door slam behind him, and what may be laughter. In my hand is a crushed scrap of paper; I did not feel him place it there. I wonder at his confused loyalties. It is a letter, an explanation of sorts, you did not even sign it; oh cruel woman.

My darling, I cannot come with you. I cannot leave my husband, I cannot leave my country, I cannot leave my faith.

Cannot? Why can you not; when I have left all these things and more for your sake?

Why tell me this? What do I care for your wedded lord? What care have I for my erstwhile country? What should I care for church or state if you would only come with me? But no, you will not come.

I stare at the lightless window of your self made prison. Was it you I saw there, mocking me; grieving?

I will not believe it. You would not let me go so easily. You say you cannot go with me? Well then, can not is not the same as will not – who dictated this letter for you to write?

But no, it is true. You cannot come.

What would you do, Ebba, if you went with me? An outcast in a strange country, a heretic, my mistress? No; it is better that you stay here among the snows and woods and learn to freeze your heart, as you must; as I never can.

You must learn your comfort, such as you may find, for what solace can there be in eternal separation? I have lost you, but you will never lose me, even when I die I shall love you.

How is it I can turn my back? How is it I can make my feet move – why am I not already dead?

There is no life left for me, I shall live only in your memory. Each step I take takes me further away from you, from life; how shall I bear it?

Todd leads your horse away as I arrive alone. He does not question, and that tells me enough of what he thinks of you, and of your faithlessness. John says nothing, loyal silence, but his stiff back as he mounts says, *We thought this would happen.*

I am raw and broken, and his generous silence, his pity wounds me. I have cast away my shield, thinking you would sustain me; now I have no protection, and no purpose. How can my life have meaning?

The horse moves out of the gate without my prompting, following the lead of the other horses. Gathering speed, the wind in my face, anger fills my lungs and I whip the horse, racing at full stretch down the road to the sea, the road to freedom, that must now, forever, be my exile. This is not the escape I hoped for, it means nothing without you, and now it is too late to change my mind. I can never return.

Well – I will never see you more. Well – you prefer safety to me. Well – and what of it? There are other women, many women who would be glad to share my life. There is a whole world out here, Ebba, full of women –

So why is it I fear they will all seem frozen and lifeless after you? As frozen and lifeless as I feel?

Do not destroy us totally, by putting me from your mind. Hold me in your memory.

Goodbye beautiful one –
remember
your Christina.

THE BONE BOX

Once there was a man living in the world who was so tall and broad that the people around him thought he was a giant, although he wasn't. There were no giants left, except those in the sea, who sometimes sing in the manner of humans.

So the man who was not a giant lived among his fellows, and thought himself better than any of them because he was taller and broader. And because they were a little afraid of him, no one told him that they were every bit as good as he thought himself.

The name of the man who was not a giant was Fulke, and he loved only two things in life. He loved to stride the hills and open spaces, and he loved to make and solve all manner of puzzles. He would play chess with anyone who would try him, and always won. Best of all, he liked boxes. Not ordinary boxes, but the kind that are carved from a solid piece of wood, like three dimensional jigsaws, the kind that have secret openings that can only be found with much ingenuity.

Because he thought he was too good for the ordinary people about him, Fulke had not taken a wife as men generally do, but he wanted one, and often looked about him in search of a woman as fine as himself.

So Fulke played chess and worked puzzles and strode the hills and looked for a wife. And when he was not doing the things he loved, he worked at building houses, which he liked tolerably well.

Now, in the world, as well as mortals there were elementals. There was Rockwoman, who weighed down the earth to stop it floating up to meet the sky and there was Windwoman who stopped the sky from falling to meet the earth. There was Treewoman who clothed the earth, and Rainwoman, who fed the rivers and trees of the world. Then there was Moonwoman who turned the tide, and Sunwoman who warmed the Earth. Finally there was Earthwoman, who just was.

And the man who was not a giant thought that as no mortal woman could be his wife, he would have an elemental to be his bride. So, between building houses, he strode the hills looking for an elemental and his thinking was this: even he could not expect to marry Earthwoman, nor Sunwoman nor Moonwoman; but Treewoman, or Windwoman or Rainwoman were within the bounds of his imagination, and he meant to have one of them within the bounds of his house, and as quick as might be.

So Fulke strode the hills looking for his wife to be. He never saw Treewoman, because, as he moved all the time and she stayed so still, she was never quite where he looked. But Rainwoman and Windwoman were another matter. They went almost everywhere together, for Rainwoman loved Windwoman, and was loved by her in return. They flew about the world hand in hand making storms and showers and breezes as the mood took them. They would rest together on high mountains, clothed in cloud, and they would lie in each other's arms and sleep.

One could always tell where they were; thunder shouted it, lightning pointed the way. So Fulke followed, waiting to catch a glimpse of the elementals, until one day, climbing a mountain, he saw clouds coming and ran and ran to reach the highest point hoping to see inside the clouds as they passed by.

And as luck would have it, Windwoman and her beloved Rainwoman were tired, and stopped on the mountaintop. The cloud settled all across the peak like a broad brimmed hat.

Fulke cowered behind a rock and stared as the mist

thinned and Rainwoman and Windwoman stepped from the cloud, arms entwined, and settled into a mossy hollow to sleep.

Windwoman was black as night, her skin soft as velvet, her long, long hair was the colour of cloud, white and fluffy, and floated about her. She put her arms protectively about Rainwoman, and kissed her fondly before they settled down to rest. Rainwoman was the colour of ice and the planes of her skin set rainbows dancing across the mountain. Her long, long hair was dark silvery grey and hung heavy about her, except when Windwoman stirred it into a torrent of glory. Rainwoman nestled into Windwoman's arms, and kissed her warmly before sinking into her dreams.

Fulke gazed at the sleeping elementals and knew he wanted Rainwoman for his wife.

As Rainwoman lay asleep, all unknowing, he crept from his hiding place and crawled towards her. Trembling at his own daring, he reached out to caress her.

Windwoman's eyes snapped open, and he stared into them. It was like staring into the eye of a hurricane. Swirling, violent, unknowable depths swung out to drag him down, drinking in his soul. A blast of air as strong as a falling wall knocked him down and away, sent him tumbling down the side of the mountain.

Windwoman gathered up Rainwoman and called the clouds together with a great crash of thunder to show how angry she was.

Down and down the mountain fell the man who was not a giant. Thunder crashed above him, lightning struck to one side and then the other, until at last, Fulke fetched up at the door of his very own house.

For a long time he just lay there, too frightened and bruised to move. At last he got to his feet and found that Rockwoman had been kind to him; nothing was broken. If she had known, Rockwoman would have crushed his skull. Still, he was too bruised and stiff to work on the house he was building for his neighbour and he lay in his bed and brooded for several days over how he might make Rainwoman his wife.

Fulke knew that he could never have her while Windwoman stayed at her side, protecting her; so he thought and thought until he at last decided on a plan to capture Rainwoman.

The man who was not a giant went away, leaving his neighbour's house half built and without a roof. Even with his great long legs to carry him he travelled for many weeks. At last he came to the place he meant to set his trap.

It was a very flat place with no hills for the two elementals to rest upon. He came to this flat place and he began to build.

He built a huge round tower with walls as thick as three men standing shoulder to shoulder, so that his tower would be too strong for Windwoman to blow down. Inside the walls he built a stairway so that he could carry the stones up to keep building higher and higher. And as he built, he covered the outside of the stone with copper, so that the lightning Windwoman would throw could not rock the tower, but would sizzle harmlessly into the ground.

There were no windows in the tower and only one doorway. It had to be a very large doorway for Fulke enter.

At last the tower was finished and all that was left for Fulke to do was to find a door for his great doorway. There were not many trees near this barren plain, but at last he found a great old oak tree. He pulled it up by the roots and carried it back to his tower. Then he set to and sawed and hammered until he had two great doors, all covered with copper on both sides. One of these he hung on the great hinges in the great doorway. The other door he fixed to the top of the tower.

And then the man who was not a giant sat down to wait.

He did not have to wait long. It was a long time since there had been rain in that barren flat land. Windwoman and Rainwoman did not like to go there often because there was no high place to rest. And, as the tree that he used for a door could have told him, they were due to visit. It had set its seed in readiness, and now its acorns were spilt all over the threshold of Fulke's tower.

So Windwoman and Rainwoman came to the barren land and Windwoman carried Rainwoman slowly across the great expanse of the plain to make sure the earth was well watered. This tired them both, and they were so grateful to find somewhere to rest, that they settled onto the tower that Fulke had built without wondering where it had come from.

Up jumped Fulke and caught hold of Rainwoman, pulling her down into the tower, slamming shut the tightly fitting door he had built.

Windwoman screamed and roared outside the tower, but she could not get in. Rainwoman beat at the underside of the roof door, but she could not move it. Fulke waited. Windwoman threw thunder and lightning at the tower, but the thunder rebounded, and the lightning sizzled down into the ground. Rainwoman beat at the door at the bottom of the tower but she could not move it. Rainwoman sat down and wept.

Windwoman called to her beloved, but Rainwoman was too upset to answer her. Windwoman could hear her weeping.

Windwoman called out,

'Who is in that tower?'

Fulke trembled. Rainwoman stopped her sobbing for a while and looked around. No longer blinded by fright, she saw him for the first time.

'There is a man,' she answered her beloved.

'Then make him open the door.'

Rainwoman looked at Fulke, and Fulke looked at

Rainwoman, hardly daring to believe he actually had her within his walls.

'I do not think he will open the door,' said Rainwoman. Fulke folded his arms and nodded at her.

'Then I will blow down his tower,' said Windwoman. Rainwoman looked at the walls.

'I do not think that you can,' said Rainwoman, and started to cry again.

Windwoman roared and thundered, but the tower did not so much as shake.

'I will not leave here until you are free,' shouted Windwoman. But Rainwoman did not answer.

Now, in the world, there was a woman who was rather cleverer than most. The name of this woman was Adamanta, and she was born of a daughter of Rockwoman, with that family's stubbornness. Now Adamanta had never married, finding no man who could match her cleverness. So, to keep herself amused, and to help her find a soul companion, she had learnt a great many languages so that she might talk to animals and trees and the like. She was very broad minded, as well as clever.

So, when the rain season came and went with no sign of Rainwoman, and never a breath of Windwoman, Adamanta knew there was something wrong.

Adamanta did not hesitate. She packed her travelling bag, put on her good coat and her walking shoes, locked her house up and went to see what had happened. As she travelled she asked each of the peoples she met when they had last seen Rainwoman. The most accurate answers came from the plants and amphibians, who worried more and noticed when Rainwoman did not visit.

Eventually Adamanta found the great plain. Right from the very edge she could see the great, tall tower, gleaming pale green from its copper covering. She could hear Windwoman's rage and Rainwoman's grieving. Now that she knew where they were, Adamanta settled down to rest for the night. Windwoman did not sound like she was planning on going anywhere, so Adamanta might as well get a night's sleep and be fresh in the morning.

Sunwoman rose and stretch lazily across the morning sky, warming Adamanta and waking her.

'Good morning Sunwoman,' she called, even though she didn't think Sunwoman could hear her. Adamanta made herself a light breakfast, put on her shoes and set off for the tower. She made good time, having started early and being a strong walker.

'Good morning Windwoman,' she called.

'Good morning?' roared Windwoman, 'and what do you think is good about it?'

'Well perhaps you will tell me what is wrong with this morning?'

'Wrong?' shrieked Windwoman, 'Rainwoman is being held prisoner in that tower, that is what is wrong.'

'I see,' said Adamanta.

Windwoman looked down at the woman.

'Seeing it doesn't help much, I want it changed.'

'Yes,' said Adamanta, nodding, 'that is what I am here for.'

She walked slowly round the tower, peering at it. Windwoman followed, hovering impatiently. Adamanta looked at the tower and thought about asking her grandmother, Rockwoman, for help. But her mother had always said that her grandmother had strange ideas about what kind of help to give, and only to ask if she was desperate.

'Well?' Windwoman asked, as Adamanta reached the door for the second time.

'Excuse me,' Adamanta said, then, clearing her throat,

addressed the door in woodspeak.

'Good morning door. I hope you don't mind my calling you door, but unfortunately I can't see who you are under all this copper.'

A rather muffled voice answered.

'Oak, pleased to make your acquaintance.'

'Tell me, Oak, are you copper covered on both sides?'

'I am afraid so.'

'I see,' said Adamanta. 'I don't suppose there are any of your Acorns about?'

'Well, yes. There are several just beside me on the inner threshold of this tower. One of them has even started to sprout, with all that crying Rainwoman has been doing.'

'Good,' said Adamanta. 'I want you to call Treewoman here. It is most important that you do.'

'I will do what I can,' said Oak, 'but its very difficult when you are smothered in metal.'

'I would appreciate it,' answered Adamanta, and settled down to wait.

Treewoman was some time coming, she was not in the habit of speed. Adamanta passed the time talking to the tower, first in Ore, telling the copper what it was being used for; and then in Stonespeak, explaining to the rocks from which the tower was built the reason for their placing. Although it took all Adamanta's powers of persuasion, at last she got their grudging agreement to her plan. She was, after all, a granddaughter of Rockwoman.

So, when Treewoman arrived, Adamanta was more or less ready for her.

Treewoman greeted her sister, Windwoman, and called out to her.

'Where is Rainwoman, your constant companion? I have saplings in need of her.'

‘Excuse me,’ said Adamanta quickly, before Windwoman could launch into a long account of her woes, ‘but we need your help. We need to get this tower apart somehow. Oak has a few acorns beside her which are sprouting, and if they could be given the strength to grow quickly, they could help prise the rocks apart.’

Treewoman looked at her, a little surprised to be addressed by a human.

‘Do as she asks,’ Windwoman breathed, suddenly believing that there might be a way to free Rainwoman.

‘Of course I can help,’ said Treewoman, ‘but what about this man who thinks he is a giant? I have seen him, he is clever and crafty, and handy with an axe. I do not think he will just sit by and watch my acorns grow.’

‘No,’ said Adamanta, ‘I do not think he will. But I have heard about him. He loves a good riddle. I will climb up onto the roof, and I will ask him riddles. That will keep him busy.’

And without more ado, she got out from her pack a little pickaxe. And with the pickaxe she made a small hole in the copper coating on the wall of the tower, just above the first line of stones.

‘Excuse me,’ she said first in Ore to the copper, and then in Stonespeak to the rocks beneath. And then, making holes to cling on to, she began to climb.

While Adamanta had been travelling to the tower, and while she had been waiting for Treewoman, Rainwoman had been trying to reason with Fulke. She had tried reproaching him for his trickery, and his cruelty in separating her from her beloved Windwoman. She tried to make him feel guilty about all the places that were not getting the rain they needed to survive. She tried to make him feel sorry for her by crying. Nothing worked. Fulke had what he wanted, nothing else mattered to him. Of course, without the light of Sunwoman, no rainbows fell from Rainwoman’s skin, and her hair hung dully about her without the breath of Windwoman to lift it. There was no getting away from it, locked away from her proper place, Rainwoman was no longer beautiful. Her skin was hard and cold to the touch, and she was damp to be about. Fulke had developed a terrible cold.

Fulke had expected Rainwoman to give in and agree to be his wife. His supplies of food were getting low. But Rainwoman would not agree.

Adamanta climbed the walls of the tower; and into each little hole that she made with her pickaxe, she placed a seed. When she had nearly reached the top, she reached up with her pickaxe, and swung it forward, but it did not bite into the copper, and she slipped and began to fall.

Without thinking, Windwoman scooped Adamanta up and deposited her on top of the tower. Adamanta was out of breath with shock, or she would have shouted at Windwoman, who could have carried her to the top of the tower in the first place. Just for a moment Adamanta thought about crying off and leaving Rainwoman in the tower. But without her pickaxed holes, she could not get down from the tower unless Windwoman carried her. When she had her breath back, she rapped on the wooden roof of the tower and called out.

'Hello in there, Giant, I have a riddle for you.'

A muffled voice answered her.

'Who are you, and why are you here?'

'My name is Adamanta, and I am the cleverest woman in the world. I am here because I heard you are the strongest man in the world, and I have come to challenge you to a duel.'

'My name is Fulke,' came the answer, 'and I will not come out of my tower, so I cannot accept your challenge.'

Now Adamanta had never imagined Fulke would be so stupid as to come out of his tower. However, he clearly thought she would think it, which showed that he was already underestimating her. Adamanta stamped her foot irritably.

'I don't want you to come out of your tower, I wasn't planning a wrestling match. I have a riddle for you.'

'That's not fair. As you are challenging me, I should have first go at asking a riddle.'

Adamanta smiled. Fulke's voice was louder, he had come up the stair to be just the other side of the door.

'Tell me your riddle,' Adamanta called, and they began their duel.

All the while, the acorns on Fulke's threshold were growing and pushing their roots between the stones of his walls. For three days and three nights Adamanta and Fulke swapped riddles. And while they talked, Adamanta sat on the roof and carved a little box from the knucklebone of a true giant, the now extinct dragon. To tell the truth, she was a little worried that Fulke would tire of the game before the trees had finished their work. So, she took longer than she needed to think of the answers to his riddles, keeping him waiting until he was jumping with impatience, then answering him and asking her next riddle all in the same breath. She was very tired and hungry by the time she came to the last of her riddles, as the sun set on the third day.

'What lives within a cage of ivory, clothed in streaming scarlet, and never stands still in all its life?'

Now Fulke had never heard this riddle before. Neither had Adamanta, because she had just made it up. She waited, listening to the silence.

'I could always give you a clue,' she offered.

'No, no, I don't need any help.'

Just then Adamanta heard a gentle cracking sound. She peered down over the edge of the tower and saw that the Acorns, out of loyalty to their mother, Oak, had lifted the great door away from its hinges with their spreading roots. Adamanta smiled; she had not thought of that. Quickly, to cover the noise of the door opening, she called out to Fulke.

'Have you thought of the answer yet?'

'I think you have tricked me,' shouted Fulke. 'I do not think there is an answer.'

'Oh there is,' answered Adamanta.

'Give me a clue, then,' Fulke demanded.

'You admit you aren't as clever as me?'

'Yes,' Fulke said grudgingly, just as Rainwoman slipped out of the door and ran to the arms of Windwoman.

'Very well,' said Adamanta. 'The clue is, I have one.'

'That's not much of a clue.'

'Well, there it is.'

Adamanta watched as Rainwoman was carried up into the sky in her lover's arms. She smiled as a gentle shower washed her face, and watered the seeds she had placed in the holes of the tower wall. And then she remembered that she could not get down from the tower without Windwoman to carry her down. She stamped her foot angrily.

'If you don't get the answer, you have to let me into your tower,' she said.

Fulke muttered to himself.

'There is no reason why you shouldn't let me in,' Adamanta said, 'your door is wide open.'

Fulke let out a cry of rage.

'You have tricked me, you have let Rainwoman free;' he shouted as he ran down the great stone stair and out of the door into the rain.

Fulke was furious. He would never have an elemental for his bride now. But at least he had got away without being punished for his attempt.

He looked up at Adamanta, who had beaten him at his favourite game, trapped at the top of his tower.

'Stay there,' he shouted, 'stay there 'til you rot.'

Adamanta stamped her foot, and threw the bone box at him. She missed, and it landed at his feet. Fulke picked up the box and turned it over and over.

'A bone box,' he said, 'an ivory cage! Whatever is in here is the answer to the riddle.'

He shook the box; there was no sound. But then, hadn't Adamanta said that the thing was wrapped in scarlet clothes? It would not rattle. Fulke sat down on the step outside the door to his tower and started to work out how to get into the box.

Adamanta watched, and wondered how she was going to get down from the tower. She remembered what her mother had told her about Grandmother Rockwoman. She looked over the edge of the tower at the nearest of her footholds. It was too far down. Adamanta decided that she was stuck, and that she was hungry, and she was prepared to risk her grandmother's strange ways of helping her family.

So she upped and shouted for her grandmother. Three times she shouted, and as soon as the last word left her mouth, the tower gave a great shudder, and began to fall to pieces. Adamanta shut her eyes tight, until the shuddering had stopped. When she opened her eyes, most of the tower was still standing, but she was sprawled on the ground, right next to Fulke, and he didn't even raise his head from the bone box.

Adamanta stood up and dusted off her clothes.

'You won't find what you are looking for in there,' she said, and set off for home.

The man who was not a giant turned the box over and over, trying to find a way in. But there were two things he did not know. One was the answer to Adamanta's riddle, and the other was that Adamanta had not finished the box, and there was no way into it.

In time, the acorns Fulke had dropped and the seeds

Adamanta had planted grew and pulled down the rest of his tower.

They say Fulke is still sitting there puzzling over that bone box. He has forgotten that he ever wanted a wife, and does not know that Rainwoman has had her revenge. He has grown so thin and still, sitting on the step of his shattered tower, that only the ceaseless movement of his heart trapped in its ivory and scarlet cage tells him he is still alive.

MEMBER OF THE FAMILY

It is a Sunday afternoon and the visitors are arriving. Angela is in the hall, rattling keys and gloating over the number of cars churning up the gravel of the drive, which isn't really a car park – all the more to buy her home-baked teas later.

She hasn't opened the door yet, it's only 2.27 by her digital watch, although the grandmother clock (French, eighteenth century, notice the interesting painting on the face and the upside-down numbers), struck the half hour two minutes ago. Of course, she (as always) is right.

I pin my 'guide' badge on and struggle up the steep staircase (mind the third step, it's not the same height as the others). I rest at the top, ready to 'do' the upper floor as required by the more inquisitive type. I don't 'do' as heavily as Angela – I can always hear her droning on downstairs, boring their ears off.

I don't know why she always gets to do downstairs, it's me who has trouble with my rheumatics, and she doesn't really know the first thing about it. Well I do know; she says it's so she can keep an eye on the kitchen and her cakes, but really it's because she doesn't feel comfortable 'doing' the bedrooms.

2.30 – the door opens to an impatient shuffle of card showing, coin rattling, umbrella shaking and stiletto shedding. In less than five minutes the ones who can't cope with Angela will be up here, hoping I'm not going to lecture them. I watch them over the banister rail.

The literary types are peering dutifully at the very dull books in the glass-fronted case in the alcove, and the manuscript (unfinished) in the display case just far enough from the door for security.

The architecture buffs linger over the carvings on the staircase, entwined mermaids; that's why they lived here, because of the mermaids.

The gardeners glance round impatiently and head for the back door, the conservatory and the garden, despite the drizzle.

The *I'm-a-member*'s finger the pottery and wall hanging, ignoring the 'do not touch' sign – which cannot possibly apply to them.

The *raining-on-holiday*ers are complaining that it's not very big and you'd have thought someone that famous would've lived somewhere, well – grand, wouldn't you, and regret having parted with the £2.50 they could have spent at the cinema if they'd known.

Those *in the know* are blocking the stairs, gazing intently at the photographs: Sarah smiling into the sun, shading her eyes; Clare asleep in a deck chair. Sarah with a dog; Clare gardening in her father's old cap; Sarah and Clare on holiday with an unidentified friend. Of course, I could identify the friend, but I don't think she'd be very pleased. Then there's the one of Sarah and Clare mending the car, or trying to – the car that they were driving when – well, that car.

Now the first of them have reached me. A tweed-and-shootingstick couple with grandchild (bored) in tow. Rained off life-members at a guess. They look expectantly at me, so I smile. He comments on the cartoon at the top of the stairs. I hate that cartoon, Clare hated it, Sarah hated it, even Angela hates it, but there it sits, because it's 'historically valuable' just to remind you that people hated them, in case you hadn't realised.

I am part way through my witty exposé of the scandal that was responsible for its existence, when I see their eyes glaze, although the child is looking more interested, and realise I've said something wrong. I find myself trailing off, saying – of course, don't let me keep you from seeing the rest of the house if you aren't interested – and imagine Clare making evil eyes at his hurriedly retreating back and throwing imaginary daggers at him. I wonder what it was they objected to.

The next group is hovering, not wanting to be told the official version. Seven or eight women, one of them clutching a sheaf of hand-written notes. They look hopefully at me, willing me out of earshot so that the note bearer can give her lecture in peace. I oblige, but not without an exaggerated favouring of the left leg that is not entirely necessary. I seat myself in the window where I can hear perfectly: there is nothing wrong with my hearing.

They cluster around the doorway to the bedroom and she starts to tell them what little she has managed to glean from the guarded comments that have been published from Sarah's notebooks – Clare never wrote a thing. There are no letters: you don't write to someone you share a bed with every night for thirty odd years.

It's amazing how little they left behind. One best seller of notoriety, three notebooks covering everyday things for about six years; lots of photographs, a small country house with an interesting garden, the odd letter to friends; the unfinished manuscript. That's about all.

I can hear the lecture unfolding along somewhat wishful lines. I walk gently back to them and interrupt. One or two visibly jump.

'I'm sorry dear, but that's not correct at all. An interesting theory, of course, but it is complete nonsense.'

She glares at me with the 'and what would you know about it' expression. So I trot out my credentials: sister of the author, co-benefactor under the will, part owner of the house. She bristles, and I bet she's thinking I've got loads of letters hidden away, but I haven't. So I explain that it is not true that Sarah had other lovers, that she and Clare were boringly monogamous (sorry to disappoint); Rachel was my friend, and certainly never slept with Sarah. One of them laughs. I warm to the subject, ignoring the faintly shocked silence that seems to have fallen over the rest of the house, and even raise my voice a little.

I tell them about the walking holiday Sarah and I had gone on in 1938, and how Sarah had tripped Clare up going into a tea shop, in her urgent haste for something hot and wet.

I tell them how she had been rude to Clare's husband Malcolm and then made me apologise for her. How Clare had copied our address down from the inside flap of my bird watcher's guide, without saying anything, and written to us –

'Ruby darling, you're causing a terrible blockage on the stairs,' calls Angela in one of her anxious 'don't be so obvious' voices, terribly bright and cheerful, threatening terrible things later.

Of course she is right. I wave them on, suggesting that Angela's teas are worth a try, and they take the hint.

It happens regularly. There are always some women who really want to know. So I tell them. But I don't tell them about me. Sarah's the famous one, the dead one, the one Clare chose. We are entitled to some secrets in the family still, I hope. Poor Angela would have a fit if she actually discovered that I had more in common with Sarah than being her sister. After all she's only related by marriage.

It's strange how much I miss them still, Sarah and Clare. Especially Clare. That's partly why I still do this stupid guide business. Where else is a woman my age, living in the middle of nowhere, going to meet other Lesbians?

LADIES' PLEASURE

The moment Grace had dreaded most had arrived. She had put away her belongings and she had waved off her daughter and son-in-law. Then she had made a restorative cup of tea, washed up the cup and put away the tea caddy and crockery in the cupboard in the tiny area that served her as a kitchen.

And now, unless she was to appear standoffish, she must put on her cardigan, and her distance spectacles, and go into the communal lounge.

It reminded her a little of her first day at boarding school, so many, many years ago. But then she had been sharing a room, and been able to share her fears and that first step into communality with Rosa, who had also been new.

But this was not school and it was her child she had waved off, rather than her mother. And there was no other home to go back to. Consequently, it was pointless to be homesick. Grace knew all of this with a cold detached rationality, but she was, pointlessly, homesick. She was homesick for her rather dreary flat in Mitcham, with her noisy neighbours upstairs. She was homesick for the constant traffic to and fro outside her door. She was homesick for her tiny garden, despite the pot plants and geraniums she had with her. And most of all she was homesick for her cat, Flossie, who now lived with her daughter.

Grace found tears prickling her eyes at the thought of Flossie uprooted, without her, trying to hold her own in an alien and unwelcoming environment. Of course, Audrey would look after her. And she, Grace, would be able to visit, at weekends; like being in hospital, or prison.

They were both doing a life sentence now, with no

remission for good behaviour.

Grace allowed herself to cry, in the vain hope that it would make her feel better. She had to admit, reluctantly, that she was giving in to her desperation, her anger at having allowed herself to be persuaded, bullied, into a home. Well, not a home, a sheltered unit. The only difference being that she had her own kitchen and shower room (no bath, in case she slipped and drowned herself).

Grace had never had a shower before, but she suspected that the novelty would wear off regrettably fast.

She blew her nose, wiped her eyes and glasses, and looked in the mirror. It was obvious that she had been crying, but she was past caring.

She straightened the Celtic brooch on her cardigan as though it were a medal, and opened her door.

In fact it wasn't as bad as she had feared. There were only a few people in the lounge. A small group of women around the television with the sound up so loud that they were oblivious to all else. An old man playing patience at one of the tables. A woman smoking at the open window, in the misguided belief that this would prevent the smoke from distressing the others. The light breeze swept the smoke across the room and Grace coughed reprovingly.

The smell was reminiscent, distinctive. She hadn't smelt that particular blend of tobacco for – it must be over fifty years, except once or twice. She knew it at once. A particular, very expensive cigar. A smell she associated with her youth. She refused to allow herself to remember why.

She settled nervously into one of the hard, high backed, vinyl chairs that, for some reason, the authorities believed to be appropriate to the needs of the elderly.

Elderly; she really couldn't use that description for herself. It was absurd. Of course she couldn't deny her age. She couldn't pretend she would see seventy again. But she didn't feel old. Certainly not old enough to be consigned to the indignity of cheap bus fares, queuing for a pension, being referred to by cheeky youngsters as a wrinkly and being forced into a dumping ground for the elderly.

If she was honest, she knew she needed the support available, but she had hoped for a flat of her own where she could have kept her cat. Not that there were rules against keeping cats here, but Flossie was used to her garden. It would have been cruel; but was it any kinder to have abandoned her to Audrey? Grace knew that she could eventually get used to living without Flossie, but she was not sure she could get used to living with the guilt.

Grace rubbed anxiously at her reading glasses, swapped them for the distance glasses she had been wearing, and pretended to read the May Sarton she had brought from her room.

That was another thing, nowhere for her books. She had carefully labelled boxes under the bed filled with the books she couldn't live without.

After what seemed like a decent interval of shared space, Grace carefully replaced her bookmark, swapped glasses, and returned to her room.

No one had made any attempt to speak to her. She did not know if she felt relieved or aggrieved. She checked her watch. She would go for a walk; just around the block, it didn't matter where, just away. She needed to prove to herself, to remind herself, that she had a key to the main door and could leave whenever she wanted.

A week passed and Grace established herself, and something approaching a routine. She still felt unacknowledged in the lounge, although one or two regulars would smile accommodatingly at her when she entered, clutching her book. She knew that she should make more effort, but did not feel equal to it. They had, as far as she could tell, nothing in common but their extreme age, and a level of decrepitude sufficient to persuade the council that it would be ill advised for them to be housed in the isolation that, for her part, Grace craved.

Still, she knew it made sense. She had had a mild stroke and although she had recovered, she had been shaken and badly frightened by the experience of lying helpless for hours, until the upstairs neighbours turned off their stereo for long enough to hear her cries for help.

The humiliation of having her front door broken in, and poor Flossie terrified under the fridge; she knew she couldn't bear that again.

When the young woman from the housing department had come to visit, and explained about sheltered housing, it hadn't sounded too bad; but the reality – it was like being buried alive; and with about as much chance of rescue.

Grace had a visit from her granddaughter, who looked pale and unhappy. She found that despite her own misery, she still worried about Julie. She'd always felt they had a special relationship, that Julie told her the things she couldn't bring herself to tell her mother. Grace found Audrey hard to talk to, and was not surprised that Julie suffered the same way.

Over two cups of tea, Julie nerved herself to tell her grandmother why it was she looked as though she hadn't slept in days.

The cause of her granddaughter's distress was, Grace discovered, that her boyfriend, Greg, had left her. Their mortgage, which relied on both salaries, was in serious arrears, and her home was in danger of repossession. And, as if that wasn't enough, Greg had left her for another man.

Instead of looking shocked or censorious, Grace nodded in sad acknowledgement, as if not greatly surprised, and then offered her granddaughter a warm and substantial shoulder to cry on. While Julie cried, Grace remembered.

*

During the war she had been stationed at an airbase, as a radio operator. She had fallen hopelessly in love with a young American pilot called Vincent. He had been inseparable from his friend, Jack. Grace and her friend Enid had made a regular foursome with the young pilots for trips to the cinema, the pub; nothing serious. When Enid had left the airbase, she had continued to keep company with the two men, causing a certain amount of talk among the few other women on the base. Grace had ignored the talk with difficulty. She had felt that she was perhaps getting more than her share of male company, but neither of the pilots showed the slightest interest in finding another woman to make up the numbers.

Although Grace had been intoxicated by Vincent's sheer physical beauty, it was Jack she had felt easy with, able to talk to. Perhaps because of the lack of intensity in her feelings, perhaps because Jack had been willing to make the effort. Vincent had made no effort. It was as though her worship had flooded over and around him without making the slightest impression. Whatever the reason, Grace had found herself more and more in Jack's company, Vincent becoming more and more distant, impervious, uninvolved. Although neither of them had admitted it consciously, most of their talk had been of Vincent. Jack's life had revolved around him, he had worshipped him. Grace's ardour had been no less total. Their mutual enthusiasm had engendered a liking between them, which at length became passionate: although she had loved to dance with Vincent as often as she could, Grace had always reserved the last dance, the slow, romantic dance, for Jack. She could not have borne to be so close to the untouchable glory of Vincent.

So while Jack trod on her feet and held her close, Grace had watched, with a feeling of exquisite sadness, Vincent standing at the bar. She watched for a twinge of jealousy, but she watched in vain. Vincent would smile benevolently, drink off his whisky, and lean on the bar, watching, with his hands firmly in his pockets. At the end of the night, he would kiss her in an apparently casual, but too accurate way, on her left cheekbone. Always the same spot. And then he would turn away, leaving Jack the more passionate embraces. And when Jack had finished his goodbye kisses, he had always run to catch up with Vincent.

Grace had tried to pretend she did not know, but she had known: She knew that Vincent had been completely impervious to her because he was in love with Jack; that his studied indifference had hidden jealousy, not of Jack, but of her.

But it was not a consummated love. And so, because their emotional entanglement with Vincent had gone nowhere and needed outlet, she and Jack had turned to each other, and gradually became lovers. Grace would lie in Jack's arms and imagine he was Vincent, and if, occasionally, she had suspected that Jack imagined the same, she refused to let it disturb her.

And so it would have continued if Jack's plane had not been shot down over the North Sea.

It had been Vincent who came to tell her; who held her while she wept. And it was she who held him while he wept, longer and harder than she had done.

After that she hardly saw him. But, a few weeks after Jack's death, she discovered that what she had suspected was true; she was carrying Jack's child. The silence between them was no longer tolerable. She had sought him out, waiting outside the Mess to catch him.

He had been terribly drunk. She was afraid that he had been drunk for the whole four weeks. When she told him exactly why she had come, that she had no one else to turn to, he had laughed; and then he had cried. Grace had waited and seen the look in his eyes as he suddenly understood. He hated her. She had regretted asking him, then. But Vincent would not let her bring the child up alone, in disgrace; it was Jack's child.

They were married by special licence, and spent their wedding night lying stiffly apart in the double bed. After the ritual kiss at the end of the ceremony, Vincent had never touched her.

Vincent had rapidly become careless and reckless, ruthless in his flying. He impressed his superiors, but terrified his fellow flyers. Grace watched him go with dread, watched him return in grateful relief; she was not surprised when at last he succeeded in killing himself. She never knew what precisely had happened. It made no difference. He was gone.

*

So no, she was not surprised about Greg.

Grace felt sorry for Julie. She remembered how it had hurt to acknowledge that Jack loved Vincent more than he loved her, and that Vincent loved only Jack. But she'd had a long time to get over the hurt, and she was glad for Greg. There must be a way to resolve Julie's financial problems. They talked for some time. Eventually Julie left, a little comforted and more able to face telling her other relatives that Greg was no longer a part of her life.

Grace felt lonely when Julie had gone, and for the first time, went to the lounge without a book under her arm.

The smell of cigar smoke greeted her. Its warmth made her feel better despite her disapproval. The woman with the cigar was at the window once more, staring into the garden. On the paving slabs outside, a cat chased the first falling leaves with ponderous dignity. Grace laughed, and then felt a terrible pang of misery for Flossie. The cigar woman turned her head and glanced at Grace.

'D'you like cats?' she asked abruptly.

Grace nodded, not trusting herself to speak with the threat of tears so close.

'Used to keep a cat. Died three years ago,' the woman said.

Grace nodded again. The woman ground out the cigar butt on the window ledge.

'New aren't you?' she enquired.

It reminded Grace of being interrogated by the prefects on her first day at school.

'Yes,' she said submissively.

The woman pushed her glasses further up on her aquiline nose.

'Smoke?' she asked.

Grace shook her head. The woman took another cigar from the breast pocket of her jacket, and a small pearl handled knife from her skirt pocket.

Grace hadn't seen a knife like it for years. They had been common once, but the one she remembered had been specific, and went with the smell of that tobacco. She glanced at the face concentrating over the cigar, frowning as the first puff of bluish smoke wafted into the air.

The woman inhaled deeply and then puffed a small smoke ring. And that too was familiar. Pretentious, Grace thought, with one part of her mind, while another part raced about the warren of her memory for a name.

The woman pocketed the knife and lighter.

'Keep a cat?'

The part of Grace's mind that had been searching files, flew back to attention. She explained with a shaking voice, about her beloved Flossie. As she spoke, the craving for Flossie's small, warm body winding confidingly about her ankles became overwhelming. She decided to visit Audrey as soon as she could.

The woman smoked in silence for a while.

'I've got a ground floor room with a door onto the garden,' she said slowly, cautiously. 'If we asked, I'm sure we could swap rooms, and then you could have your cat back, couldn't you?'

Grace was stunned. Apart from the possibility of having Flossie back, this complete stranger was offering to disrupt her life for her. She didn't know what to say; but her mouth opened, and spoke an emphatic yes, without her consciously willing it.

'I like cats,' her new friend said, by way of explanation.

'I don't know who you are.' Grace said, suddenly remembering social niceties, if not quite fulfilling them. The woman laughed.

'I'm Jessica Markham.'

Grace's mental filing cabinet flung itself open. Of course she was Jessica Markham. *The* Jessica Markham. There could hardly be two, especially not two cigar-smoking Jessica Markham's.

'I knew a Jessica Markham once, at school. You didn't go to school at Leybridge did you?' Grace asked, not quite ready to admit she knew this woman.

Jessica acknowledged that she had; a wicked, somewhat toothless grin spread across her face.

'And you still remember? I must have become famous without realising.'

Notorious would have been closer to the mark. Jessica Markham had been famed for bucking the system, unlike Grace who had, by comparison, been an obedient and nauseatingly virtuous child. Jessica had claimed to be a communist, stayed out late, smoked and drank. There had been the famous time she danced the Tango at the end of term dance.

How she had danced. Grace had always longed to dance like that, to dance with Jessica Markham, who had been quite stunningly beautiful.

Then she remembered who had danced the Tango with

Jessica. Rosa.

'So, tell me who you are.' Jessica suggested.

' I used to be Grace Carew,' she replied without thinking. Jessica laughed.

'And who are you now?'

Grace smiled, and thought that she really wasn't the same person she had been all those years ago. Not that she was planning on explaining that to Jessica.

'I got married during the war. I only meant I had changed my name.'

'I avoided that trap, thank god,' Jessica said.

She always had been a rebel, Grace thought, almost affectionately. Thinking of endless misdemeanours, thinking almost without being aware of it, of Rosa.

'You always were a rebel,' she said, and somewhere between thought and tongue the meaning had twisted, becoming bitter and angry.

Jessica's eyelids drooped and the glance she shot Grace was hurt, and careful and distant. She ground out her second cigar butt and did not answer, but she too, thought of Rosa.

Yes, she had always been a rebel. She nodded, gently, almost kindly.

'Yes, I was,' she said, 'and you were no slouch in that direction, I remember. What about Rosa? Whatever became of her?'

Grace, in turn, became guarded.

'You don't know?'

'No,' Jessica said, suddenly feeling her age, not wanting to hear, knowing from Grace's tone that whatever had happened to Rosa Neale had not been good.

Grace could be generous; she shook her head.

'This isn't the time or place,' she said. 'Do you still want to talk to the warden?'

Reprieved, Jessica was glad of the change of subject. She was always glad to do a cat a good turn. She wasn't so sure about Grace, but she grabbed Grace's hand and hauled her away to talk to the warden.

And that would have been the end of it, had the spectre of Rosa not hung between them. Reunited with her cat, Grace might have reduced her contact with Jessica to a grateful nod of acknowledgement when they coincided in the lounge; Jessica, once she had been introduced to the ungrateful and timid Flossie, might have withdrawn to her solitary smoking by the window. But the uncomfortable knowledge lurked, making Grace speak to her old enemy, her old rival, her old idol. They spoke of nothing; safe dull topics which could be ended if they strayed too close to their shared past, to Rosa.

Grace, knowing the power of the information locked into her filing cabinet memory, was more careful than Jessica; whereas Jessica had curiosity always there to tempt her to take risks.

So, when Jessica saw the notice informing residents that the local school was going to provide a musical entertainment, she sought out Grace, full of *do-you-remember*?

'Do you remember we used to be forced to sing Christmas carols to the old biddies from the town?'

Grace remembered. She also remembered that she was an old biddy now, and resented the youthful patronage of the local school. She could manage without their musical entertainment.

'They probably think we like *Goodbye Dolly Grey*.'

Jessica laughed.

'You mean you don't?'

'I shall go out until it's safe to return.' Grace replied. Jessica became impatient with her.

'It will be funny. Besides, it will be pleasant to see an

attractive young person in this place, never mind dozens of them,' she said, leering a little.

Grace shook her head. Jessica was playing her games again, pretending to be an old reprobate, when she was just another dull old woman incapable of looking after herself any more. Jessica read the look, and bristled angrily. Pointless – she had discovered already that she couldn't intimidate Grace as she had done when they were young. She surveyed this woman who ought to be a friend, who was determined to be a stranger.

'What was it I did to you at school that was so terrible?' she asked at last.

Grace thought about it. She imagined a dusty file stamped *Private, Confidential, Top Secret,* the way she had marked her schoolgirl diary. Not that it had stopped her mother reading it. Grace shook out the folds in her memory.

Jessica waited, sensing that if she was patient for once, she might hear something important.

Grace's courage failed her. She shrugged.

'I can't remember.'

Jessica stomped over to the window, flinging it open, letting in cold damp air. She fumbled with her cigar, knife and lighter. She wouldn't mind if she could only remember herself. She couldn't think of anything particularly dreadful she could have done to the young Grace. She scarcely remembered her. But then, she had been so casually cruel when she had been young, it would be easy to forget some slight injury to an insignificant brat.

Jessica did not believe she had ever done anything really awful, but the headmistress had not seen her endless misdemeanours in the same way, and Jessica had eventually succeeded in getting herself expelled. Her parents had been very angry. Not with her, with the headmistress. There had been an almighty row. She had listened, although she was supposed to be summoning up an appropriate remorse.

Jessica smiled, remembering her younger self, equilibrium restored, and then she remembered what that row had been about. She ground out the cigar and looked round for Grace, to ask her something that now seemed urgent; but she was gone.

Neither of them attended the school's entertainment. Separately, they sat in their rooms, isolated from the world and each other. When the next poster appeared, Jessica did not discuss it with Grace.

Grace, however, was seduced by the poster. A tea dance. She hadn't danced for years. She longed for the confidence dancing always instilled in her body.

The dance was to celebrate the hundredth birthday of one of the residents. On enquiring, Grace discovered the birthday boy was none other than the man who always sat in the lounge, playing patience. Grace hoped most devoutly that she would not live to be one hundred. However, a party seemed like a good idea, and there was to be a live band. Something approaching excitement gripped the residents, all except Jessica, who had discovered what it was she had done to Grace, and could find no way of explaining herself.

The tea dance was all too raw a reminder to Jessica of her faults. The terminal row at school had started with a dance; she had tangoed with Rosa Neale and that had just been the beginning. More importantly than that, Jessica had remembered the shadowy figure dogging Rosa's footsteps all those years ago. The inconvenient girl who shared Rosa's room, who had to be shaken off all the time. When she had been expelled, and Rosa had not, Jessica had thought the shadowy Grace had won that silent battle. Now that assumption was in doubt, and she could not think of a way of broaching the subject.

The dance was not a success. The inhabitants of retirement

homes, however sprightly, are almost all women. For the majority of the residents, therefore, there was a problem. Mr Docherty's younger male relatives did the best they could, but most of the residents sat patiently, disillusioned, magnificent dowager wallflowers. The band were mediocre but competent, the sherry sweet. Grace was angry with herself for wanting the party to be fun, to be a success. *This is the price of growing old,* she thought bitterly; *nothing is fun anymore.* She sat uncomfortably in her best frock, and gazed miserably at her fellow prisoners. They would be better off with some kind of party game or folk dancing, reminiscent of holiday camp holidays with Audrey. At least everyone could join in.

At school there had been no boys, and the girls had naturally danced together, waltzing, quickstepping, whirling about in their dancing pumps and flowery dresses. During the war there had always been more women at dances than men, it had become acceptable for women to dance together; but then they had been in uniform, somehow anonymous, as though justified by rationing and austerity fashions, an acceptable substitute for the real thing, like margarine.

Here, now, these women who were mostly the same generation as herself, who must have done the same things as she had, could not bring themselves to dance together. Grace tried to work out why. Was it the glittering Lurex two-pieces that inhibited them, or the presence of the younger men? If only one couple were to make a sedate turn about the room bosom to bosom, surely it would make it possible for the others?

Grace looked about. There was no one she felt she knew sufficiently well, and why should she take responsibility for the first move? It wasn't her party.

A hand rested lightly on her shoulder. Grace looked up and round. Jessica smiled down at her, doing her best to banish the worried frown that wanted to take precedence on her face.

'Would you like to dance?'

Grace nodded. How many times, she wondered, had she waited for Jessica Markham to ask her that? How many times had she hoped to be chosen, and been passed over? How many times had it been Rosa instead, a double blow to her unspoken longing?

Grace stood carefully. She stepped out to the middle of the floor, Jessica at her shoulder.

The band played a waltz. That was safe, easy. They had spotted the two women, were letting them ease their way into the dancing.

Grace felt conspicuous, felt heat rising to her face. She had not danced with a woman since school, except for dancing with her daughter occasionally at family functions, when Audrey was very young. Even the war years had not brought her a woman dancing partner, cushioned as she had been by Jack and Vincent. It made her uneasy to think of them as a protection against the possibility of women.

Grace concentrated on Jessica. She was wearing a magnificent 1920s beaded dress. She really has kept her figure, Grace thought. She remembered that dress. It was black, chiffon, virtually transparent over a black silk slip that made it respectable, just. Tiny glass beads were sown all over it, in swirls of flowering vines, out of which grew tiny Chinese dragons. It even had a beaded fringe, which was losing beads at every step.

Grace listened to the tiny rattle as bead after bead hit the highly polished wooden floor. She wanted to stop, to try to pick them up. Jessica held her hand, firmly and danced on, smiling.

'Don't worry,' Jessica said,'This is definitely the last outing this dress is getting. The seams are all rotten, it won't make it to the end of the night.'

Grace felt sad. That dress had been something in its time,

a symbol of Jessica's outrageousness. The Tango dress.

'I think it's time I told you,' she said.

Jessica shook her head.

'Not now. I do remember what it was I did. I'm sorry, but I never meant to hurt you.'

'No. But only because you never thought about me at all.'

Jessica missed a step, shuffled a bit to catch up.

'Well. Obviously I'm in the wrong again – or is it still?' she asked resentfully.

'Never mind,' Grace replied, shaking her head. 'Dance.'

Grace smarted under Jessica's surprise. But after all, what had she expected? It was perfectly true that Jessica had never thought about her, so why should that suddenly have changed? She hadn't thought much about Rosa either, or she would know what had happened.

The band risked a foxtrot. Jessica looked round, there were two more female couples dancing now, although there were also several disapproving faces. She smiled. The party had been rescued from its emotional constipation. Now she would see what could be done about Grace. She wasn't sure why she was bothering. Perhaps it was just that she had discovered it would be nice to have a friend, especially one who remembered her prime, so that she could bask in remembered glory. The trouble was that Grace didn't seem to remember it like that. Grace remembered her as a troublemaker who had hurt her by taking her girlfriend. Or so Jessica surmised. What was it that had happened to Rosa since that had been so terrible, and why did Grace think her responsible?

Jessica decided to ask. She didn't feel comfortable dancing with Grace, not with this silence between them.

'What really happened?' she asked.

Grace sighed, she didn't want to have to explain now, the moment had gone. Despite her reluctance she began to tell her, still dancing. It made her a little breathless.

'Rosa went crazy. That's what they said, anyway. Last I heard she was failing to dry out in a home for hopeless alcoholics.'

Jessica felt her spirits sinking. It wasn't as though she and Rosa had been the only girls at the school who went further than holding hands. Even some of the staff had been more involved than they would care for the parents to discover.

'And you hold me responsible?'

Grace shook her head. It wasn't as simple as that. She had lost Rosa, certainly, but it was never Rosa she had really wanted. And whilst she would have liked to blame Jessica for Rosa's subsequent downfall, she knew that Rosa's parents, and the school, had played a greater part in that particular disaster.

'No. Your only mistake was to be too public, you made it an issue, so that they had to do something about you. They threw you out, but you had the easier path. Rosa had to stay and face the scandal. She wasn't any good at it, not like you would have been. You know how cruel children can be; you know how cruel you could be. We all shunned her. Me too, I won't pretend. I was scared they would think that Rosa and I did the same –'

'Didn't you?' Jessica looked disbelieving, 'I thought that was the whole point, that you and Rosa were together.'

'No. You made that impossible.'

Jessica snorted disbelievingly, angry.

'So it was my fault.'

Grace felt she was not saying what she meant any more, that she was allowing Jessica to shape her words for her. She refused to answer her.

The band was warming up, getting adventurous. Jessica made to move back to the safety of the seats, leaving the floor to the few mixed couples, the increasing number of younger, more daring women.

Grace kept hold of her hand, refusing to move. Jessica smiled, one of her evil grins. If Grace Carew-Petrullo wanted to dance the Tango, then she was more than willing to give it a go. She was glad she had warmed up with the other dances first, her back wasn't as supple as it had once been.

Grace felt the gentle-firm touch of Jessica's hand on the small of her back.

My god, she thought, *is this what I waited nearly sixty years for? Is this it?*

She was disappointed. When all was said and done, it was only dancing, however risqué. This was not the dangerous, delightful, desirable moment she had always imagined. All she had ever wanted to do was dance. With Vincent, with Jack, with Rosa, but first of all, and most of all, with Jessica Markham. And here she was, dancing. There was definitely something missing.

It feels wonderful to be dancing like this again, Jessica thought. *Invigorating, exciting, daring*. She whirled Grace's portly figure about, and started to stalk towards the doors of the lounge, Grace crushed to her. She laughed: it was ludicrous, really. Making an exhibition of herself, that's what the headmistress had called it. She had done more than that, when she had danced with Rosa Neale, much more than that. Even that school wouldn't have expelled her for just dancing. Jessica was caught up in the memory of it, she had been dancing like this, cheered on by the laughing horde of girls, dancing close and hot and excited, and she had danced Rosa out of the school hall, up the stairs and into her bed.

Rosa had been tall and willowy, not stodgy like Grace; but actually, Grace danced better. Grace danced beautifully. She liked dancing with her. Jessica suddenly noticed that she had lost the lead, that Grace had usurped it, and was leading her firmly, gently, towards the doors. She looked down at Grace, who was looking extremely determined. Well, she thought, smothering her surprise, enjoying having her bluff called. She allowed Grace to bend her protesting back into a swoop down to the floor. It alarmed her a little, she wasn't sure she would make it back up. Another shower of beads cascaded off her dress. Jessica laughed.

They reached the doors. Grace pushed through them, and they swung closed, muffling the music. Grace let go of Jessica's hands, a little out of breath, a little out of her depth.

'So what happens next?' she asked, anxiously.

'More dancing,' Jessica said.

*

Next morning, Grace's bed was full of little glass beads.

HOLIDAY ROMANCE

Dear Mary,

I heard from Mrs Amis about Geoffrey's death, and am writing to express my sincere condolences. I hope it hasn't hit you too hard. I wanted to offer you my hospitality if you feel the need to get away for a while.

It's time bygones were bygones, please write and let me know if you can come. My very best wishes,

Frances.

I hand the letter back over the teapot to Mum. It is almost like a voice from the grave, getting condolences so long after my father's death. The more so since he hadn't been part of our lives for far longer than the three months since he died.

'She obviously doesn't know you've been divorced twelve years. How come I've never heard of her?'

Mother doesn't answer immediately, so I ask my next question on the tail of the last.

'What does she mean, bygones?'

'Well we haven't exactly spoken since I married your father.'

'That's a long time to not speak, what had you done?'

'What makes you think I was at fault?'

'Well, were you?'

She hesitates, as though thinking about how to apportion the blame.

'Yes,' she says, finally.

'So, what had you done?'

'Married Geoff.'

'Oh I see, pipped her at the post did you?'

'Something like that,' Mother says evasively. She takes off her glasses and puts them in the toast rack, along with the letter.

'Well, are you going to go?'

'Of course dear. I shall write immediately, but I don't think I should stay with Fran in the circumstances. I'd better go to the hotel.'

I pick up the letter and read the address. It is the small cliff top town on the east coast where my great-uncle lived until he went into a home. I have never been there, although I used to write dutiful family letters to Joseph Callum at Christmas, and birthdays. Suddenly the idea of the North Sea seems appealing.

'Can I come?'

'Why on earth would you want to do that?'

'I haven't had a holiday, and if you aren't going to stay with the noncommunicative Fran, I could come too.'

'I suppose you're leading up to asking if you can bring Teresa.'

Mother has hit a sore point here. Sore with me, as well as with her. She doesn't like Teresa, and still resents her as an interloper. She refuses to be reconciled to the fact I live with Teresa even after three years. However, my reasons for not bringing Teresa with me are not to do with Mother's attitude.

'I might have,' I say, 'but, unless there's been a sudden change of plan, Teresa's cycling round the Pyrenees or somewhere with Roberta.'

'Oh, so that's why you're here. Teresa's off with the 'other' woman.'

'She's entitled to friends of her own,' I say virtuously, although Mother is, in fact, right. I am trying to be adult about it, to pretend I don't mind that Teresa has, in effect, deserted me for two months; it is proving harder than I expected.

Mother takes the sports page out of the paper because it

won't stay in, and snorts. I hope she is going to leave me alone, or at least be sympathetic if she's seen through my attempt to cover up my romantic difficulties. I would like to be able to tell her what I really think, but her hostility to Teresa gets in the way; it feels disloyal to admit Teresa's failings to someone who is so determinedly against her.

'So while the cat's away playing, the mouse falls back on her poor old Mum for company,' she says, choosing to be unkind, a habit she has only recently acquired. We used to be close, and generous with each other's failings. Not any more, but I still try even when she throws my attempt at reconciliation in my face. I treat it as a joke; maybe it was.

'Poor old nothing. It's not my fault if all my friends are rich and go abroad for months on end.'

'I don't see the connection between those two statements.'

'Nor do I, but I'll think of one, something to do with poverty I expect.'

'Meaning?'

'Beggars can't be choosers?'

'Me or you?' Mother asks archly. The effect is spoilt as the business page falls into the marge. I change the subject.

'It took her a while to find out.'

'Took who a while to find out what?'

'Frances, about Dad.'

'I see. I thought perhaps we were still on the theory of relative deprivation. Yes it did, but then it would. No reason why she should ever have known, really. Geoff's family don't live there any more.'

'Why didn't you tell her?'

'Lost her address, or rather – well, actually I didn't bother.'

'That's not very nice after pinching her lover.'

'I did not pinch her lover. The print in this paper is dreadful, I can't read it.'

'Put your glasses on, dope, and don't change the subject.' She doesn't put on her glasses. She favours me with a rather vague frown, but stops trying to change the subject.

'Look sweetest, if you must know, Frances and I parted over twenty years ago, with her screaming that she hated me and then running her car into me.'

'I thought you said your legs got damaged in an accident,' I say indignantly. It pisses me off when she invents dramas.

'It was an accident, she meant to kill me.'

'Oh come off it, Mother.'

'Well she was rather cross, you know,' she says, in a somewhat conciliatory tone.

I think about it. Mother has never, ever, referred to her injury in my hearing. Except for once, when I was very young, young enough to need to be met from school. I had been being teased all day by one of those little knots of bullies you get at primary schools.

Melanie's Mum's a man, she always wears trousers; Melanie's Mum's a cripple, Melanie's Mum's a witch; watch out she doesn't hit you with her stick.

On and on, until I had gone to hide, with all the other cowardly, put upon children, at the back of the shrubbery.

I had been ashamed to run up to her in the playground at home time after that, and for days I'd continued to hang back, before I would allow her to find me, and take my hand to walk home.

Eventually she'd got round to asking what I was upset about.

'What's a cripple?' I had asked; I already knew what a witch was. She'd looked at me, and I hadn't been sure if she was going to burst into tears, or slap me. She didn't answer my question, but she told me what she felt I needed to know.

'Look, sweetest, before you were born, I had an accident.

So now I need a stick to help me walk. That's all there is to it.'

I'd wanted to ask her if I could look at her legs, but it seemed impossibly rude, so I'd nodded, ever so solemn and grown up.

'I expect it hurts,' I had said.

'Yes. Yes, it hurts.'

We never talked about it again, and now suddenly she shows me a letter from the woman responsible, and proposes to visit her. Frankly, I think she's crazy.

I play the scene in my head, like a fifties movie. Eastman colour, vivid blue night sky, violent red sports car. Mother played by Jean Simmons, Frances in a yellow full-skirted dress, played by Kim Novak. Hitchcock directing. Dali-esque camera angle, music too loud, the roar of the engine exploding through the score and the blood red scream. I can almost smell burning rubber. I pull myself together.

'How do you know she doesn't harbour homicidal tendencies to this day? I'd better come with you to be your bodyguard.'

'Don't be ridiculous, Fran wouldn't hurt a fly. Yes, you can come, yes, I'm going to go, and I still can't find my glasses.'

I get the distinct impression she is hiding something from me. She doesn't usually make such quick decisions.

Although I was joking about the bodyguard business, the habit of acting as my mother's protector is hard to break; I've always fancied myself in gleaming silver armour, riding a white horse, the whole Knight Errant thing; with my Dad as the dragon. So now, a new dragon; if she's telling the truth about the accident. It makes me uneasy. If it is true, why would she want to renew contact with this woman, and why does she think it is safe to do so?

I hand Mother's glasses to her and she abandons the paper to find her writing pad and organise this trip into the past.

Somewhat to my surprise, Mother doesn't change her mind. A week later we are turning out of Railway Approach at Tidesmill, me struggling with my suitcase and Mother's, she holding a large straw hat firmly on her head in the gale force wind.

My cats are in the charge of the neighbours, the papers and milk have been cancelled, and the week ahead is ours for the taking. Mother knocks coke cans aside with her stick and does things-ain't-what-they-used-to-be at me as we cross the road, although, to me, things look very much as they must have been when she was last here. We head for the 'Cliffview' guest house, which is a converted lifeguard's watch house and is not as twee as that sounds. This is where Mother stayed the year she met Dad, when he was on holiday from university, and she was accompanying an ageing aunt who thought a fortnight of sea air would do her good. It didn't and Aunt Lucy died on the last day of their stay, thus giving Mother an excuse to hang around longer than she might have otherwise. I know all of this, it is in the authorised version of family history. Now there seems to be an unauthorised version, too.

The Cliffview is under new management, so there is no renewing of acquaintance after twenty-odd years. Mother seems faintly disappointed at this, as am I. Despite the change of management, the place is stuck in such a time warp, that it must have been old fashioned even when mother was first here. I feel like an alien in this sort of environment. No wonder we never visited Uncle Joe; it is not a desirable spot.

Still, I had been hoping for a little local insight into this whirlwind romance that so nearly ended in disaster, and it no longer seems likely that anyone here will remember. Of course, depending on how you look at it, my parent's romance could be said to have ended in disaster anyway. In my opinion, the biggest favour Dad ever did my mother was to leave her.

We unpack, and Mother prances about deciding what-to-wear-to-meet-Frances, in an uncharacteristic flurry of frivolity. I decide not to go on this first exciting rendezvous, despite the urge to lurk behind Ma in a trenchcoat, with a discreetly obvious .38 (or .45 or whatever they are) in my pocket. Well you never know. Even libraries in small coastal towns can harbour killers.

Mother is due to meet Frances at the library when it closes and then to go for lunch at the Red Lion Inn. I try to persuade her to come for a walk on the beach first, but she refuses. When I see the acres of shingle I understand why.

I try to skim stones over the waves, and fail. Grey waves, grey stones, grey clouds. I find myself imagining Roberta and Teresa on their tandem, freewheeling down some heady mountain pass in hot sunshine. I have them crash at the bottom, but it doesn't make me feel better. I know perfectly well that if Roberta were to collapse at my feet, I would resuscitate her. I am not like this Frances woman. I don't drive at people I don't like. Not that I can drive.

It is of course pure coincidence that after my bracing stroll by the sea I decide to have a quick half in the aforementioned hostelry at just after two. No, it is not coincidence. I just can't bear my own company any longer. The wind has not died and I suppose I look rather more disreputable than usual, which might account for the strange looks the locals give me.

My eyes adjust to the dim light and I see Mother's bright green jumper in a corner. She's sitting with her back to me and Frances (presumably) is facing me. She gives me an appraising look, which makes me think I've met her before. She is Mother's age, but doesn't look it the way Ma does. She doesn't look as though she would suffer from fits of jealous rage, or drive the sort of souped-up sports car I had been imagining.

She doesn't even look like an ageing Kim Novak. I'm not sure if I am reassured, or disappointed. Apparently Frances doesn't think me worthy of her attention, her eyes flicker away, back to Mother. She looks bored. I take my beer and ploughperson round the other side of the bar and consume them rapidly. On a visit to the ladies I see they have gone.

I saunter slowly back to the hotel revelling in the blustery wind that would almost hold me up if I leant on it.

*

Mother is sitting on the end of the bed looking glum.

'How'd it go then?' I ask brightly, pretending not to notice.

'Awful,' she says, kicking her shoes across the room.

Not a good sign that. She continues, 'I couldn't think of anything interesting to say so I gabbled on about Geoffrey.'

My mind boggles at what she might find to say about a man who treated her the way he did, and at Frances's possible reaction to her revelations.

'That was a bit tactless,' I say, then bite my tongue.

'Tactless yourself,' she replies, with some justification, 'I couldn't help it; I opened my mouth and all the nonsense just poured out. It wasn't even true, most of it.'

'Oh, Mother.' I know this sort of mood. It hits me sometimes. At least she can confess her idiocy to me. It ought to make her feel better, it always has done before; but the newly built bridge over the distrust between us is still tenuous, and I have to tread carefully.

'Well I don't know what to do now,' Mother says, attempting a light tone, and failing. 'She thinks I'm a tactless half-wit and that being married has addled my brains, and I daresay she's right, and we're here for a whole week, and what on earth we're going to do in this dump all that time I can't think.' She bursts into tears.

I am exasperated. I am not used to my mother acting like a moon-struck schoolgirl. She usually has more dignity.

I don't know what she expected; after all, she hasn't seen the woman for over twenty years, only knew her for a few weeks and pinched her boyfriend. What on earth is she so upset about? What exactly are we doing here?

I reflect that Mother's analysis of what Fran might think of her is too close to what I think and feel disloyal. After all, she is my mother and, despite that drawback, I love her.

Mother blows her nose loudly and mutters 'sorry' into her handkerchief. I pat her ineffectually on the back.

'Now you've said all the nonsense, do you think you could have a rational conversation with her?'

'I don't know,' she says, dispiritedly, 'she just sits there, all calm and polite and like it never happened. I keep thinking I ought to apologise, and I don't want to. I wish we hadn't come.'

'I think it's her who should apologise.'

'Why?'

I tap her walking stick gently, the lightness of the touch at odds with the fierceness of how I feel. Last time Mum was in this deadend town, she could have walked on that shingle. I could really hate that Frances if I put my mind to it.

'That's different,' she says rubbing her eyes raw. 'She was angry, and she didn't mean to.' She sounds a little better now, as though she might make sense if prodded far enough. I prod.

'And?'

'And I was cold blooded, deliberate, stupid, and I didn't care if I did hurt her, and I feel awful about it.'

'So tell her.'

'I can't!' she wails, dissolving into another howling fit. She refuses to respond to entreaty, threats or sympathy. I've never seen her so upset. After snivelling into the eiderdown for a bit she staggers off to the bathroom.

I decide to try another source of information. I go to the library.

The place is tiny compared to the libraries I'm used to.

Two interlinked rooms, one fiction, the other non-fiction, with the catalogues and issuing desk forming an L shape in the middle where a menacing looking begonia takes pride of place. There is a step down from fiction into non, which seems to sum up the priorities of the librarian; non is much smaller.

There is a door marked 'private' leading out of non, and I assume that Frances is out there, as there is no-one in either of the visible rooms. I scan the shelves. Holiday reading mostly, local history, customs and the like. Boring.

Frances appears through the private door, with a pile of very new books, some of which are still leaking shredded packing paper. She dumps them on the desk without noticing me, and sits down. I put a book back on the shelf as loudly as possible, and she looks round.

'Hello, I didn't see you. Were you looking for anything in particular?'

'Yes. You.'

She looks puzzled.

"I'm sorry?'

I walk over, imagining myself in a Raymond Chandler movie.

Ok Blue Eyes, gimme the low down on why the dame is acting so – queer.

'I'm Mary Callum's daughter.' *Cue dramatic swirl of music.*

This is the point where she's supposed to leap to her feet with one hand to her throat and stammer guiltily. She doesn't. She picks up one of the books and a catalogue card.

'Really,' she says.

I wonder what to say next.

'Mother's upset.' I say lamely.

'Is she.'

'I want to know why.'

'I really have no idea.'

I try again:

'She was really looking forward to seeing you and she thinks she's made an idiot of herself.'

Frances finishes writing the card and puts the book to one side, picking up another.

'Does she.'

'Yes.'

'And what do you want me to do about it?'

She looks up at me and her eyes fix on my lesbian badge. I cringe a bit, the time warp feeling of the place is beginning to get to me. Frances goes on staring, then shuts the book with a snap.

'I really don't see that it's any of your business. If you don't understand why your mother and I have nothing in common, that's your problem.'

'You invited her down here.'

She stands up.

'That was because I thought there might be something worth salvaging: there isn't. Your father made sure of that.'

'That's less than fair.' She has me rattled. I can't remember the last time I felt like defending my father's reputation.

'Your father,' she says, her voice tight, angry; 'was a nasty, voyeuristic, dishonest, violent, sadistic –' her voice starts to tremble and she stops speaking.

'My father,' I respond angrily, 'was a prize shit, but he never did anything to Mum that was half as bad as what you did.'

She takes a deep breath, forcing herself back into control, and speaks very quickly.

'I am not interested in your opinion; now please – go away.'

I decide to leave. I feel like crying. It doesn't happen like that in the movies. They're supposed to crack and tell all.

I storm out into the street and go to the Post Office to send Teresa a postcard, even though she isn't there, and one to the cats, care of the neighbour. Something about the name across the window rings a bell. Amis. I can't place it. I leaf through the postcards until I find one that isn't too hideous for the cats, and the tackiest possible for Teresa. I feel almost normal by the time the woman behind the counter turns her smile on me, which freezes a little as she gets a good look. I tell her I want stamps, but she continues to give me searching looks. I wonder if she suspects me of shoplifting. Then she says,

'You're not a Cornwallis are you?' I know there are plenty of code names, but this is a new one on me.

'A what?' I say, although once I have adjusted to my surprise, I know perfectly well what she means.

'Cornwallis; there was a girl came here once, years ago, spit image of you, she was. I never forget a face, can't remember her first name now, came with her aunt, who died here.'

'My mother. Mary.' I reply cautiously, scenting that joy of detective writers, the busybody with a photographic memory. I didn't think they really existed, and now I've found one, I'm not altogether sure I feel like listening to her.

'That's the name,' she replies eagerly. 'Your mother? Never thought of her as the marrying type somehow. Marry anyone I know?'

'Geoffrey Callum,' I say, resigning myself to being dragged into her reminiscences.

'Of course, she was one of Geoffrey's lady friends. So they did get married then?'

'I beg your pardon?'

'Well, perhaps I hadn't better say, shouldn't speak ill of the dear departed, now should I?' she says, with every intention of doing just that and relishing it.

'Please,' I say, my curiosity getting the better of my rather feeble family loyalty. We have both forgotten about the stamps.

'Well, my ma ran the post office then, Cicely Amis, she was, she's retired now. I'm Sally. My younger sister was walking out with young Geoff in those days. Can't say I ever saw the attraction, nasty minded boy. I always avoided him.' She makes this last comment in a reflective tone, as though remembering what she had been doing instead of taking notice of my father, and she has obviously forgotten, or doesn't care that I might be offended by her revelations.

'He seems to have got about.' I say, a little wearily. Since he died, I've lost interest in counting my Father's faults, and his women. But Sally is, by implication, confirming what Frances said.

'Oh yes, quite a lad our Geoff. Then your mother came down with her aunt and he forgot all about our Ellen. Couldn't keep his eyes off her. Not that Ellen was worried; Madam Cornwallis didn't take any notice of him, and anyway she was only here a few weeks. Knocked around with that Fran Townsend, doing long distance walking and I don't know what all.'

I'm confused, this doesn't fit.

'I thought he had something going with Frances?'

'Her?' Sally Amis laughs, as though I had suggested my dad had been making eyes at the Queen Mother. 'Not his type, love.'

'So how come you didn't know they'd got married?'

'They all disappeared off on their own business after the accident. Your Ma was in hospital in Sparminster for ages, then went straight home after the trial. Geoff went back to college and he never came to visit his Uncle Joe again, poor old man, so he didn't come back. No reason for us to know he'd married your mother.'

I ponder on the ways of the world. In detective books,

they always have to wheedle every scrap of information out of the witnesses. Here in Tidesmill they tell you nothing at all, or everything they know. I remember my stamps. I buy them and go back to the hotel, determined to get the truth out of Mother, who never said anything about there being a trial.

I think about long distance walking, and weeks in hospital, and Frances saying that Dad was a sadist. We need to do some serious talking. Mother isn't in the hotel when I get there. I fulminate and wonder whether to go back to the library; I suppose that is where mother has gone. I go for an aimless walk around the town, such as it is, trying to work out where Frances lives, and worrying myself silly.

Just after five I am walking back to the hotel, and see Frances and Mother coming out of the library together. Frances pauses to lock the door, then takes Mother's arm. They cross the road and go up an alleyway I'd missed before. I find myself following, anxiously running to keep up; after all, if Frances tried to kill Ma once she could try again and alleys are notorious for things like that. Not that I'd have the least idea what to do, I'm not much use as a knight in shining armour when it comes down to it.

As it turns out, the alley widens and there is a row of five houses. They disappear into one of them. I dither about wondering what to do with myself. I go back to the main road and see Sally Amis closing the Post Office. She sees me and waves. I wave back, and wonder if there is anything to be gained from going to talk to her again, but I'm sure that she doesn't know any more than she's already told me. Then I remember why the name Amis means something. Mrs Amis told Fran that Dad was dead. Heard from Dad's Uncle Joe, I suppose, but the point is, she knew my Dad, and she knows Frances well enough to pass on the news of his death. I run after Sally. She looks a bit surprised.

'Does your mother still live here?'

'Yes, she lives with me.'

'And she knew my father well?'

'Yes.'

'Would she mind if I came and talked to her?'

Sally laughs, still a little puzzled.

'If you want to. She's not all there these days, but I'm sure she'd love to tell you all about him. Come to tea.'

'Now?' I ask eagerly.

'Yes. Why not?'

So I follow Sally to her house, and eat her food and talk to her mother, who is not as senile as Sally thinks, and has a different version again. In her tale, Fran and Mary already knew each other, and it had been Mary's idea to take Aunt Lucy to Tidesmill when she wanted a holiday. Fran and she had taken Aunt Lucy for drives in Fran's car, and gone for walks together. Geoff Callum had taken a fancy to Mary and dogged her footsteps, following her around on his motorbike; making a nuisance of himself. Aunt Lucy had enjoyed her holiday and died happy, in her sleep the day they were due to go home. While they were organising the funeral and such, Geoff had made the most of his position as the nephew of the undertaker. Mary's parents had appeared to help; Fran had faded into the background.

Then there was the accident. Fran had been reversing her car, or so she thought, but it wasn't in reverse, and the car had ploughed into Mary and Geoff who were arguing outside the pub. Geoff had jumped clear, Mary had been crushed against the wall. Mary had been hauled off into hospital; Fran was banned from driving, and went away for a few months to let the fuss die down. Geoff had gone back to college.

Mrs Amis is more than happy to dwell on the subject. Her enthusiasm is almost unpleasant. It makes me feel soiled, as though my own curiosity is cut from the same cloth as her salacious delight in a scandal more than twenty years old. When Sally goes out of the room Mrs Amis grabs my arm. I try to move out of her grip, but she holds on firmly.

'That's almost true, but it was no accident. She meant to do it, and she should have been put away for it. Grievous Bodily Harm. Kept damn quiet, that was. Terrible what jealousy does.'

'But she wasn't interested in Geoff Callum.'

'No, she wasn't. You think about it, lass.'

I think, but the thought that slides unwillingly into my mind leaves me gasping.

'You don't mean that she and my mother –'

'Never one for the boys, that Fran, if you get my meaning. Your mother's well out of it, if you ask me.'

'But –'

'Oh I know, terrible shock it must be for you, dear. Have some more tea.'

No wonder Fran went into hiding for a while. I can't understand why she came back, let alone stayed here all these years. I almost feel sorry for her, but there is still my mother's well-being to be considered. I have left her alone with a potentially dangerous woman. Cicely Amis can only have a suspicion to base her story on; if she had known anything for fact, Frances would never have come back here. For all that, her comment fits too well for me to doubt it.

I run my film clip again. *Close up on the gear stick, Frances' hand fumbling with it, unable to see what she's doing, blind with tears of rage –*

Then again, *calmly, in red this time, a sharp suit with high collar, getting the engine turning, close up of the rear-view mirror, she smiles, her foot hits the accelerator*. Enough.

I make hurried goodbyes and half run back to Fran's cottage, not at all sure what I am going to do.

Mother is just coming out of the door. She turns and kisses Fran, and it is no peck on the cheek. And I thought she needed protection.

I wait for her at the end of the alley, three years of resentment ripening to fruition in the few seconds it takes for her to reach me.

'You rotten creeping fraud!' I shriek at her. 'How bloody dare you! Putting me through all that torture when I came out to you, all that cold shouldering, and pretending Teresa didn't exist; and all the time you were lusting after that woman!'

'Melanie –'

'Shut up! I haven't finished. All that tripe about you pinching her boyfriend. He pinched her girlfriend!'

'I never said that, you did. Stop screaming at me and let me explain.'

'I don't want an explanation, I want an apology.'

'Melanie, I've just done this scene with Fran, and please keep your voice down.'

I storm along in furious silence, with Mother struggling to keep up, talking fast.

'All right, yes, I had a – a –' she flounders after the right word. I do not wish to help her out, but I fling a few suggestions at her.

'Relationship? Affair?'

Mother comes to a stop, refusing to try to match my pace, forcing me to turn back.

'Yes,' she says, not defining which of my suggested descriptions she means, 'but I have not been lusting after Frances all this time, as you so crudely put it. I've been too busy hating her.'

I take breath to answer her, to say that I don't understand what has changed; but she won't wait for me, plunging back into her story.

'I was so naïve. I believed Geoff when he said Fran had driven at me deliberately. I wanted to believe it, but I still told the police it was an accident; I had to – if I had said anything different it would all have come out at the trial. I'm sorry I was so awful to you, Melanie, but you made it so hard for me. It felt like a punishment, when you told me about you and Teresa, as though you were forcing me to remember, forcing me to think about Frances. And I didn't want to, I wanted the whole episode to be erased.'

Awful is an understatement. It wasn't just Frances she wanted to erase then, she had talked as though she wanted me erased too, permanently. She has a lot of making up to do before the feeling of betrayal goes away. I favour her with a sneer. She ignores the look, ignores the warped logic of her own argument, ignores the ease with which she dismisses her own cruelty.

'You've helped me through all that, Mel. You know I don't like Teresa, but seeing you so happy with her made me realise it might be possible to stop hating Fran.'

I wince. The trouble is, I am no longer happy with Teresa, but this is no time to say so. Mother has forgotten about the cycling tour with Roberta. I sometimes wonder if she ever listens to me.

'What are you drivelling on about?' I ask, crossly. Mother looks at me pleadingly.

'I so wanted to tell you, but I didn't know where to begin, and I felt like you had stopped trusting me, which I expect I deserved, I was scared of how you would react.'

She was scared of how *I* would react? I could laugh if it wasn't so depressing. I make an effort to reassure her, but can't find the words, having only just been vile to her. Instead, I ask,

'So what was it made you change your mind?'

'When I got that letter, I suddenly knew that Frances had never felt anything but love for me, and that she couldn't have hurt me deliberately. It was like a mist lifting.'

'Why should that letter make any difference?'

' Can you imagine the risk she was taking, writing to me after all that time? She wouldn't do that if she had meant to hurt me.'

'Then it was an accident?'

'Not exactly.'

'You aren't making sense.'

'It wasn't me she drove the car at, it was Geoff; and the car would never have hit me if he hadn't pushed me, trying to save himself.' That brings me up short. I forget I'm angry with her.

'Is that what Fran says?' I ask. She nods.

'How could he?' I find myself asking. Mother shrugs, despairing of understanding.

'I don't suppose he meant to.'

I am suddenly angry with my father all over again. It's just as well he isn't here to account for himself. Mother is snivelling now. I hand her a well-used tissue.

'And Fran could have gone to prison for it – how could I have been so stupid? I let him persuade me that what we were doing was wrong and disgusting, and he could save my soul, Geoffrey of all people.' She sniffs loudly.

'Frances knew him, of course. She saw right through him. She would have done anything to keep him away from me. If only I'd had the sense to jump out of the way.'

I try to slow her down. Without the background knowledge I have from the Amis women, I doubt I'd have understood half of what she's told me.

'Is that what Fran says?' I ask again, beginning to be impressed with Frances, who really had taken on the dragon, even if she failed. Mother will not be deflected from her tale, and continues without answering me.

'I was glad, you know; I wanted to hate her, so that leaving would be easy. I needed to find a reason to go and never come back. I succeeded in doing that, didn't I.' She turns to stare back towards Fran's home.

'I don't understand. Why did you marry Dad?'

Mother looks at me in surprise.

'Look, sweetest,' she begins.

I sigh. She always says that when she is going to tell me something she'd rather not.

'I was in hospital for months. I couldn't walk for – longer than I care to think about. Geoff visited me, every week. He took care of me. I was flattered, no other man would have looked at me, the state I was in. It was as if he found me even more attractive because I was helpless.'

I watch her face. There is a twitching muscle under her left eye. Another distress signal. I ought to make her sit down. I think about the way her legs looked, the only time I caught sight of them. She has always been so sensitive about that, never letting even me see the mass of scar tissue. I suddenly recall the way well-meaning relatives would give me copies of ghastly books with heroines who would be struck down in the prime of youth, only to walk again as a result of miracles, or willpower. Mother hadn't let me read them. They made her angry. She kept them piled on top of the wardrobe where all her silly dresses were kept, never to be worn, except by me, dressing up when I was alone in the house. I used to climb up to get the books, and read them in secret.

I think about Dad, how he could never stand the least sign of independence from either of us, how he was always so careful of Mother, telling her not to tire herself, not to do too much, not to, not to. And all the time he was off with some new fancy woman. And when Mum stopped taking his advice, and got a job and friends of her own, he left us. I feel a little sick. There is something else I need to ask her.

'Did you ever love him?' I say, dreading the answer, willing her to tell me what I want to hear.

'No,' she says, and sighs bleakly. 'What a waste of twenty-six years – apart from you, of course.'

'Oh, Mum,' I say helplessly, caught up in her misery, despite my relief. I hug her, not knowing how else to offer comfort and she hugs me back.

Then she starts to giggle. Suddenly it seems completely ridiculous. We stand in the middle of the street, the pair of us, holding on to each other and shrieking with laughter.

ROWAN'S VERSION

I want to tell you how it was for me, Emily.

It was just before Christmas, a Saturday evening. I had been wrapping your present.

There was dinner in the oven. I was sitting in the front room listening to a record, waiting for you to get back from town.

You'd been shopping, you'd phoned to say you would be late. I had turned the oven down. It was gone seven o'clock.

I was just sitting, waiting. When the record finished, I didn't put another on. I listened to the arm clicking back into place.

I hadn't turned the main light on, so that I could watch the headlights down on the main road, as I waited for you to turn up the lane.

You were very late, Emily.

I was beginning to get impatient, but I wasn't worried.

Eventually I went back to the kitchen and turned the oven off, poured myself some whisky.

Then I heard the car outside. I knew it wasn't you, because you always crash the gears when you reverse, so I was puzzled. I thought perhaps Mabel had come to call.

The door knocker made a sullen announcement. I put down the whisky glass on top of the fridge.

When I opened the door there were two people there. A man and a woman; both in police uniforms. My mouth dried up. I couldn't have spoken to save my life. I just nodded every time they spoke. When they said they needed someone to identify you, panic gripped me.

Not on my own, not on my own.

I ran back to the kitchen and phoned Mabel. The

policewoman followed me. Mabel picked up the phone and said:

'Hello?'

I just stood there.

'Hello?'

Eventually I croaked her name. The policewoman took the phone from me and told Mabel. She hung up and said that Mabel would meet us at the hospital. But you know that, she was with me when I saw you.

It was raining on the way back. Mabel drove me home. She wanted to come in, but I needed to be on my own, grief should be private.

I know she sat in her car for a while after I shut the door, waiting to see if I changed my mind. She told me to phone her if I needed company, no matter what time.

I don't need company, never have, just you; that's what I thought. But you see, I'd forgotten there would never be you again.

It's hard to explain. I just sat there after Mabel's headlights had splashed the ceiling as she turned down the lane. Sat and stared at the wall and listened to my breathing in the dark. I didn't even think, just sat.

About three my mind started working again.

That was when I realised that you hadn't made a will.

I went and found my abandoned whisky and phoned Mabel, which is why I know what the time was. She picked up the phone on the second ring.

'It's me,' I said.

'I know,' she said, 'I'll be right there.'

When she arrived I was pacing up and down, three whiskies the worse.

'It'll all go,' I said.

'What?'

'All of it. There's no will.'

She sat down rather hard and looked at me a bit odd. I could tell what she was thinking: screw loose.

'Are you sure?'

'Oh, yes. We talked about it not a week ago. It'll all go to that Peggy in London now. I'll have nowhere to live, nothing.'

It was quite simple really, I couldn't understand why she was being so slow.

'What do you want to do?'

I looked round at it all, our home.

'You've got to help me. I have to move all my stuff and all the things that matter, all the joint stuff, before they start prying.'

'But –'

'No. I'm serious.'

And that's what we did. All of it. In the middle of the night. You'd have laughed, I expect. Mabel was scared, said she felt like she was thieving. Sordid really. I shan't tell you all of it. But then there was your Christmas present. Just wrapped. Looking at us, it was, while we bundled our life into Mabel's car. We both knew it was there and neither of us mentioned it. Left it till last.

I was checking the bookshelves for anything with my name in it, when Mabel finally pretended to have just noticed it.

'What do you want to do with that?' She asked.

'Give it to Mrs H. for her bazaar.' I said, not turning.

'But don't you think..?' Mabel pondered, weighing your present in her hand. I wanted to snatch it from her, hold it to me, hold you to me –

'Why not?' I said. 'They can have a special side show: guess what queers give each other for Christmas.'

That was when I started to cry. Once I started it was difficult to stop. Whisky does that sometimes. I kept gulping air and finding I was using it to scream. After a while I was sick in the sink, while Mabel flapped helplessly. Then she made me wash my face and change my jumper.

I ended up with my face buried in her shoulder with her rocking me to and fro. But that set me off again because it wasn't her arms I wanted, or her shoulder; and she smelt wrong, tobacco and oil instead of sheep and cows.

Why weren't you here when I needed you?

Oh, I calmed down in the end; you always do, you know, otherwise you crack up. Mabel stayed what was left of the night on the sofa. She's a good woman, but it's not the same without you. I did wonder whether to go to church in the morning, but it didn't seem appropriate to go and pray for a heathen, not that they would listen to me anyway.

So I walked on the hills instead. The rain had cleared. Do you remember what you said once about being buried in a cairn on the top of Long Mynd?

They wouldn't have let you, you know. I suppose they thought a cremation would be tidy. Not that you'd care about that, would you, Em. Not a very tidy person. And afraid of fire.

Afraid.

I'm sorry about that love, but I couldn't afford a burial, and the solicitor rushed me so.

I went to see the other solicitor, you know, the one Mabel met in Shrewsbury. I asked him about my rights to a share in the farm. He didn't think there was much hope if Peggy gets difficult, do you think she will? I hope she hasn't got silly since you knew her. I suppose she's married. They're a terrible nuisance these relatives; I had to move everything. But you already know that.

But it wouldn't do, my love, it wouldn't do at all. That's our business. It's private, not for young Peggy to go fingering through and looking sideways at me.

The solicitor wrote and told her. She phoned to say she's

coming tomorrow. Silly, but I'm afraid. I hope she doesn't bring her husband with her, there have been enough strangers through here already. Or children, do you think she has children? I don't even know what she looks like. I wish you'd told me more, then I'd be better prepared. She sounded awkward on the phone.

You realise I can't afford to buy the place if she decides to sell? And if she decides to keep it, what then?

I'm too old for all this. I can't manage another upheaval.

Dearest Em. Couldn't you have arranged this a little better? If you had to go and get mangled by a lorry, couldn't you at least have signed the will? A draft copy on pink paper with crossings out and exclamation marks won't save me from the poorhouse. You always did leave things until it was almost too late; you just misjudged it this time. You wouldn't have been out at all if you hadn't left the shopping until last thing.

Dearest Em. I bet you think I've flipped, sitting out here in the cowshed talking to you. But it's not as though I expect you to answer me.

I miss you, you old battleaxe, I'd give anything for a good row about me overfeeding the animals. I expect I've been neglecting them for a week or two. They all send their regards. Dear me, I'm losing my grip. You never did like me talking about the cows as if they were people, I must be tired.

Good night, love.

*

Well, I got here, Ann, in spite of you making me miss the train. Two hours late, which meant I missed the last bus as well. Thanks, kid.

I know you wanted to come, but it's better this way, I didn't want to get your hopes up, I'd rather be disappointed on my own. After all it is fifteen years since I was last here. Anyway you have to sign on this week.

When the letter came I was really excited, it was like

a dream come true, we really can go and farm after all those fantasies.

When I calmed down from that, I started to worry. Like you said; we don't know anything about farming, what would we do for company and you'd have to learn to drive, reactionary rural bigots, dealing with solicitors, having to pretend (at least at first); all the old problems.

I didn't tell you, because you were sulking in the bath, but in spite of all of it, I want to move up here. It's better than I remember. Will you mind? Do you think you can bear it?

It's smaller than I remember, but I was only eleven then. We won't be rich after all; there's not much money, just the farm and the market garden.

You could do the books, you're good at that, not like me.

I know you think it's like Wuthering Heights, but it's not, and you can get pills for hay fever. We could cope, I'm sure we could.

Please say yes, Ann.

I'm glad I came on my own; you'd have been critical and I'd have listened to you. I've made my mind up, I'm going to keep it. I'd like you to come; I know it's frightening, I know.

On the train, I was watching the trees go past into the dark and thinking about Emily. It was like she was sitting next to me. I could almost see her reflection in the window, as she was fifteen years ago.

She had just finished her second year at agricultural college. She wasn't going back. Because her dad had died, she said, I found out later that she'd been kicked out, but no one knew why. Now I can guess, I'll tell you about that later.

I was remembering the time she took me into Shrewsbury for the day. We went round all the history, me being into all that stuff at eleven. It was good with her, I could almost smell the age of things when she talked about them. She missed her vocation if you ask me.

She took me to tea as well. I sat in a trance in front of one of those silver cake stands with three tiers and real lace doilies. Then I took the smallest and plainest cake on it. She was angry with me, told me I was on holiday and was supposed to be enjoying myself, maybe she felt I was rejecting her treat. She took the two biggest cakes off the stand and put them on my plate. I ate them of course, and she laughed at me.

We sang and ran all the way back to the station. It was sunny, August. She was pretending to be happy, but she wasn't.

I heard her arguing with her mother that evening, even though I was right up in the attic; the crow's nest she called it.

I wanted to go to the loo, but I was afraid to go downstairs.

She stormed out to the cow shed after a while, and I sneaked down and across the yard to the toilet. Then I went into the shed. She was standing in a dark corner, kicking the wall over and over, muttering. When I called her she started, and I saw she was crying. When she saw me she looked scared. She told me to go back to bed, at once. If her mother caught me wandering about out there in my dressing gown, we'd both get slaughtered. I couldn't see why she'd get in trouble, but she sounded as if she meant it. I was scared, so I went.

Sitting on the train watching the darkness go past, I felt guilty, and sorry. Em was all right; and now she's dead.

I was thinking, am I allowed to talk about Em? Do I say I'm sorry she dead, even though I've gained I don't know how many acres I've no business getting? Won't it sound insincere? And who should I tell? It's Emily I want to tell. I want to say I'm sorry for not telling her about me because I was afraid of how she'd react. Sorry for leaving it too late, sorry for making a stranger of her.

Me, trying to look respectable for the benefit of the locals, and the solicitor, for god's sake. And it didn't work anyway. You should have seen the look the woman opposite me on the train gave me. I wish I hadn't bothered. Emily would have laughed; she never bothered about looking the part. I looked ridiculous.

The taxi driver commented on it. (Taxi due to you making me late.)

She looked at me in the mirror and said,

'That's never the latest fashion in London, is it?'

Well of course not, and she knew it. She thought it was funny though; I reckon she's a dyke.

I had to share the taxi with the woman from the train. One Mrs Hardcastle, local busybody, and didn't take to me – mutual of course.

The taxi woman (that Mabel according to Mrs H) is a friend of the farm manager, Rowan. Everyone knows everyone and her business; you'd love that, I bet.

Rowan was a surprise. I'd expected a land army type, noisy and brisk, but she's rather like you, except she's about twenty years older.

She keeps calling me Peggy. I told her Maggie, and she said what did I want to sound like Mrs T for? I said was it any better sounding like a pirate. Swallows and Amazons, she said. Amazon, anyway; I said – to myself that is.

She told me straight out that Em wouldn't have left me the farm if she had signed the will. Well, I knew that. I suppose she meant she would have got it. She uses the kitchen like she lived with it for years. That made me feel like a toad, I can tell you. What in hell was I supposed to say? And she's acting odd; when I tried to talk to her about you (well, I might as well) she didn't answer, just stared at me like she was looking for something but couldn't find it. Then she just got up and walked away.

We ate and then she said she was going home, and went out, but she only went into the cowshed. She's still there.

I don't half miss you.

You will come soon, won't you?

*

Oh Em, why doesn't she look like you? I hoped and hoped she would. I wanted to have something to put in place of the terrible way you looked when I last saw you. Of course they tidied you up, but all the same –

That horrific bleak room with the fierce lighting that bleaches everything and flattens curves – I almost believed it wasn't you at all, that it was all a mistake and I could go home and find you impatiently scraping the burnt dinner out of the casserole. I held so tight to Mabel, I heard her knuckles give; but she didn't say anything. Somehow that's all I can remember now, the crunch of her knuckles, the smell of that particular disinfectant and the wild frightened look in your eyes.

I've spent hours staring at photos trying to piece you back together, trying to wipe out that look.

It's as though you're a stranger. I even found a picture of Peggy, the year she was staying here, when she was what, twelve, thirteen? She looked as though she might grow to look like you then, but she's lost it somewhere.

That was the year you were thrown out of college and I lost my job. I thought I was going to lose you too; but it was just the job, and a few friends, nothing really.

Would it have been easier to have lost you then, expecting it, than now, unprepared, with all that we have between us cut away and left adrift? I can't even remember the last time I told you I loved you. It was so unnecessary – you knew, I knew. We were confident in our mutuality, finishing each other's sentences, not needing to say – that you were all I needed, that you made me feel at one with the world.

To think I used to worry about how you'd cope without me. You should be proud of me, Emily, for not being the feeble old woman they all seem to think I am.

Peggy says she wants to keep the farm, but she has a friend in London she wants to live with and she might not like it here, her not being keen on country life. I've only just realised she said that. I wasn't listening at the time, trying to find you in her face.

I was thinking about the way you'd scream with rage and frustration if things didn't go right, and then laugh at yourself, and I found you in the dent in the kitchen door, where you threw the pliers across the yard, remember? I felt that dent, and I recognised you, as I do not recognise you in those photographs, or in Peggy's face.

It's almost as though the mark you left on our place, my place, is indelible, as though you are still here.

BABY PINK/ELECTRIC BLUE

'Abigail,' Auntie said, 'If the good lord had meant women to marry men, he'd have made them compatible. Why'd you think your mama never married your father?'

'Mu-um!' Abbie wailed, infuriated. Her mother, who was standing on a chair to reach her daughter's headdress, shot her sister a look, but forbore to intervene. She placed another cautious hairpin into the froth of white net, wobbling a little.

Aunt Marlene shifted her weight. Her feet were aching in her new beige court shoes. Her girdle was cutting off her circulation, and she was too hot in the jacket of her suit. She was damned if she was going to be the only one to suffer.

'And another thing, how is Henry going to recognise you? He's never seen you in a dress, leave alone with all those false pieces. Hair extensions, nail extensions, eyelash extensions. When that man lifts your veil, he's going to think he got the wrong woman.'

Hester dropped the handful of hairpins, as her daughter whirled on Marlene. She sighed in exasperation.

'That's enough now, Marlene, leave the girl alone.'

Marlene shrugged, hugging her handbag against her, as protection against the criticism and peered through the nets into the street below. Four doors down, on the other side of the road, Leo's family was collecting in the street, sorting themselves into the waiting cars. She had never seen the Eversons in so much formal wear. Last time she'd seen Leo Everson in a suit was at his Grandpa's funeral, when he was six.

It seemed a shame Abbie hadn't stuck to Leo, instead of going off with his friend Henry. You knew where you were with Leo, watching him grow up across the street. This Henry, who was he anyway?

Leo's father, Carl, was coming across the street. He was giving Abbie away, there not being any male relatives in the household. Running to fat, Marlene observed.

The rest of Carl's family drove off. Marlene noticed that Leo drove his eldest sister away in the brand new sports car that had been delivered earlier in the week. Marlene suspected Leo had timed the delivery to coincide with Abbie's wedding deliberately. She could not decide whether he hoped to make Abbie regret turning him down, or whether the car was a consolation for himself. Marlene went down to the street door to let Carl in.

*

Nina checked her bag. Car keys, chequebook, shopping list, credit cards, purse, disposable nappy, dummy. Looked like everything. She locked the front door, swapped the house keys for the car keys and climbed into the Metro. Thomas was safely strapped into the child seat, singing tunelessly about do-ggies. Sammy waved thoughtfully from his seat beside her.

She was later starting than she had intended. She had been sick again. And the test this morning said the same as the one last week. She'd fallen pregnant again. And then she'd wasted twenty minutes next door at Linda's, trying to pluck up the courage to confide in her, to ask her advice. She hadn't been able to do it.

She stared fixedly at the car in front of her. In her pocket she had the number of a pregnancy counselling service. She had memorised it on Thursday, when she went up town on the tube. She hadn't wanted to write it down immediately, to draw attention to herself. It was difficult in any case to scribble it down in her diary while on an escalator, even a long one. So she had murmured it over and over until she was sure she had it fixed, and written it on the corner of a tissue once she got the chance to sit down.

Nina turned the key in the ignition. She hadn't decided whether to phone yet. She was glad Dennis was away in

Southampton, it gave her time to decide before he came back, noticed her puking every morning. She didn't think she could stand another child so quickly. Thom was only three and a half, Sam not quite one. She pulled away from the curb. Before they had got as far as the end of the road Thomas was calling out to her:

'Mummy, Mummy, Mummy, are we there yet, Mummy?'

*

Marlene's hands were sweaty in the gloves. The hot weather was unseasonable, she thought resentfully. She was dressed just right for the end of September, it was the weather that was out of step. She gripped the back of the pew in front of her, thinking despite her best efforts not to, of another September, another wedding. When her sweet Dinah had wed that no-good man. She had let her go without a whisper of resentment. Watched her get all dressed up in white like a lamb to the slaughter. Helped her primp up her hair, for God's sake. And she had wanted to die, watching that sweet little thing up at the altar giving herself away, selling her soul to the devil. She had got up and walked right out of the church in the middle of the service, got in her car and hit the accelerator.

How in the Lord's name she had ever let Hester persuade her into this wedding she did not know. But Abbie was her godchild and she knew her duty. Why she was marrying Henry, the Lord alone knew. Marlene's hand's tightened on the pew back again, as a hot flush seized her. She glanced behind her at Leo, stony-faced and stiffly upright. She had plenty of fellow feeling for him. Abbie didn't love her Henry, she could tell. She was too young to be tied down, she should be running wild and free with Leo and the gang, dressing in denim and Lycra, not white lace.

But Marlene had been hugging her niece a lot lately, while she still had the right; she had felt the thickening waist. Not that it should matter, she and Hester had raised Abbie well enough without a man. She had worked three jobs, to bring in enough money for them all. She had withstood their neighbours' disapproval of Hester's unwed state, had been respectable enough for both of them. She had earned the respect. She would have helped Abbie raise her child.

But children these days, they don't know the meaning of struggle. Don't understand the joy of the hard way up, of knowing you did it in spite of everything. They just want their job, their mortgage, their nice home, how do they think that happens? No sense of adventure except for the kind that brings thrills in fast cars, like Leo.

*

Nina bit back a curse as she steered the trolley into the aisle, and found it blocked by a young man filling shelves. She couldn't reach the tins she wanted. She was about to take one from his box when he spread a protective hand over them, telling her they weren't priced yet. *Fine,* she thought, *fine. Keep the damn things.* She backed out of the aisle, swinging the trolley into someone's shopping bag. She apologised ungraciously, and was half way to the freezers when she realised that Thomas was no longer with her. She looked around frantically, trying to remember where she had last seen him. She retraced her steps, steering ineffectually through the Saturday crowds. The entire supermarket seemed to be full of small boys. She stopped at about the middle of the shop, and yelled at the top of her voice.

'Thomas!' Sammy gave her a startled look and started grizzling. She fished in her bag for the dummy and jammed it into his mouth. The grizzling died to a muffled whine. She shouted three more times before she heard an answering call. Each time she shouted she could feel her face getting hotter, her temper fraying even thinner.

Thomas appeared around the end of an aisle, clutching a comic, and a half-eaten chocolate bar. Nina's temper disintegrated. She strode over to him, grabbing his upper arm.

'Don't you ever do that again.' She pulled the comic from his hand. It was smeared with chocolate, and would have to be paid for. She threw it into the trolley. She extricated the remains of the chocolate bar from his hand, and threw that in as well. Thomas started to wail. Nina's hands were covered in melted chocolate, and she knew she had forgotten tissues. There was a crumpled excuse for a tissue in her jeans pocket. Getting it out, she smeared chocolate on the bottom of her shirt. She swore. She wiped her hands, then started on Thomas's face, ignoring his wails. She wanted to hit him so much, it hurt. Had there not been an audience of disapproving shoppers, she would have given into the temptation.

Finishing his face, she held him by the wrists while she tried to get the chocolate off his hands. Thomas decided to shriek and struggle, he hung from her hands, his knees almost on the floor. Nina tightened her grip, to a point where she knew she was hurting him, and jerked him back onto his feet.

'Shut up,' she shrieked, then her voice sinking to a whisper she added, 'or I'll give you something to cry for.'

Thomas hiccupped desperately, a look of bewildered injury on his face. She let go abruptly, dropping the filthy tissue onto the floor. She had suddenly had a vision of her mother saying the same thing, shaking her until her teeth rattled. She had always promised herself she would never behave like her mother. She was overcome with a wave of pity for her mother, understanding now what had driven her to snapping point. It was all too easy. She sweated with remorse and guilt. She was turning into a monster; a child-batterer. Her hands shook. She patted Thomas on the head, and took his hand, moulding it around the lower part of the handle of the trolley, he held on obediently.

She did not want her children to be afraid of her. She took a breath, fighting back the sob that was making her ribcage ache.

'Come on honey, Mama's sorry, but she's a little upset.

Let's get this shopping finished, and then you can ride the fire engine, okay?'

She was glad her voice sounded more or less normal. But she had broken another promise; she had always sworn she would never bribe her children into good behaviour. She closed her eyes for a moment. There were phones outside the supermarket, next to the mechanical ride that Thom so loved. She was going to make that phone call.

*

Marlene listened to the flow of words and stared rigidly at her goddaughter's back, all done up in white like Dinah. No grit, neither of them, not prepared to take the difficult road. Poor Abbie, too young for all that tied-down-ness. She'd tried to tell her, but she wouldn't take telling, just like her Mama.

They had got to the part about showing just cause, speaking now, or forever holding your peace. Marlene cleared her throat, turning slightly so that she could just see Leo. His nostrils flared a little, but he stayed sat down.

When Dinah got married, she had all but leapt up at this point to denounce her. She had almost told the entire congregation that Dinah was already married, to her. But she couldn't bring herself to do it. Not in the Lord's house. She had been so shamed by her cowardice that she had rushed out, got in her car, and driven and driven, like the road could never end.

Marlene found her feet under her, her knees straightening, propelling her out of her pew. She was surprised, she hadn't been planning on standing up. She sidled out of the pew and tiptoed down the aisle as quiet as she could. Not like for Dinah. For Dinah, she had run.

A few concerned faces turned to watch her go; putting her flight down to an excess of emotion or too much heat. She waved the usher aside and stepped out into the stagnant autumn air.

It was no good. She couldn't go through with it. She couldn't sit there and watch another sweet wild girl batten herself down and fit herself into the mould the world built for her. She perched herself on the low bonnet of Leo Everson's new car. Electric blue. Leo always was a bad boy, she wondered where the money came from for this beauty. Electric blue, electric windows, nice blue leather upholstery – and the keys still in the ignition.

Marlene slipped into the driver's seat. The boy had long legs, she couldn't reach the pedals. She took off her shoes and shot the seat forward a few notches. Her feet expanded gratefully, and rested enticingly on the clutch and accelerator. She liked the feel of the wheel beneath her gloved hands.

Why not? she thought, and turned the key in the ignition. The engine purred. Lovely. Marlene pulled the seat belt across her and wished she hadn't been persuaded into the girdle by the shop assistant. She took a furtive look behind her, threw her wedding hat onto the back seat and let in the clutch. The car turned smoothly out of the gravel drive and into the road. She opened the windows, turned on the cassette player. She drove off to the strains of Louis Armstrong and Ella Fitzgerald singing *Summertime*. She drove around the block at a stately twenty miles an hour. She was enjoying herself. In fact she was having a great time. Instead of turning back into the church carpark, she drove straight on past, gradually going faster, and faster.

*

Nina packed the car, strapped Sammy into his seat, and then walked Thomas over to the fire engine ride. There was a child already on it. Thomas pushed out his lower lip, and leaned against the wall in a pose indicating abject despair. Nina sighed.

'Come to the phone with me, Thom,' she said. 'Maybe the engine will be free when we get back.'

'Don't want to,' said Thom, glaring up from under his

eyebrows. Nina felt cold, he looked so like his father.

'Tough,' she said, hauling him after her.

He resumed his tragic pose against the wall by the telephone. Nina ignored him. She opened her bag, and fished in it for the tissue with the number on it. It wasn't there. It had to be there, it had to be. In desperation, she turned the bag upside down on the floor, and scrabbled through the contents. Thomas forgot his sulk and rooted happily through the spilled muddle. The tissue wasn't there. Nina looked at Thomas' chocolate smeared fingers, and a terrible certainty as to the fate of the tissue lodged in her gut. Somewhere on the floor in the supermarket. She scooped her belongings back into the bag. Maybe she could remember the number. She thought about it.

'Mummy, the Engine's empty now,' Thomas said in an imperious tone. She thrust twenty pence at him. He clutched it in his sticky hand, and rushed away in delight, before some other child beat him to his ride. She watched until he had climbed on and inserted the coin. He knew how to do it. He rode the damn thing every time they came shopping.

Nina wrote a number down. It looked the right shape. Time to find out if she was right. She picked up the receiver. The line was dead. She replaced the receiver very slowly. She looked over at the other phone. It took phone cards, and she didn't have one. Nina rested her forehead on the wall. She waited for the wave of fury and despair to pass. It didn't. There was another phone outside the post office. Thomas was shouting at her again, from his perch on the fire engine. She looked in her purse. She walked quickly over, put another twenty pence in the machine, and gave Thomas another one.

'I'm going to the post office, don't go anywhere with anyone but me, okay?'

Thomas nodded. She wondered if he was paying attention. She wasn't sure she cared. She ran out of the car park, and into the road.

*

When Marlene had left Dinah's wedding she had driven for miles, aimlessly circling, until she calmed down, found a road she recognised, and headed for a bar. She had got roaring drunk, and ended up dancing with a woman she had never met before. What it was to be young and wild. Nothing else had happened, except she had passed out. That was before she had really accepted religion and been redeemed. It didn't seem so long ago now, nor so far removed from her present life.

It occurred to her that now that Abbie was married, Henry could take responsibility for her. Marlene would be able to give up one of her remaining two jobs, take some time for herself. She was momentarily grateful, but then the price Abbie was paying came rolling back into her brain, and she couldn't be glad.

Marlene wasn't concentrating. She almost didn't see the woman step off the pavement at the crossing. Her reactions were in fine fettle, the brakes efficient; she didn't hit her. Close thing. The woman's hand hit the bonnet and she vaulted backwards with the car, landing lightly on her feet. Her face loomed at Marlene through the windscreen, frightened and surprised. Marlene couldn't help laughing. She hadn't been expecting this sort of car to be driven by the likes of her. She looked a little closer at the woman. She looked as though she had been crying.

'Sorry,' she called, 'would you like a ride?'

The woman laughed incredulously. Marlene wasn't sure what had prompted her offer. The woman stepped away from the car uncertainly, then smiled. What a sweet smile. Marlene leant over and opened the passenger door. The woman got in. Marlene offered her hand.

'Marlene Culver,' she said,'where to?'

The woman clasped her hand, smiled that sweet smile again.

'Nina Yates,' she replied, reaching for the seat belt; 'Anywhere.'

Marlene grinned. She revved the engine, she put down the handbrake and she drove.

*

Nina lay back, revelling in the newness of the car, the comfort of the carefully moulded upholstery. She was still shaking from the shock of the accident. Now that she had time to think about it, she was quite impressed by her reaction. She hadn't ever thought of herself as athletic, or even quick on her feet. She had jarred her shoulder quite badly vaulting like that, which spoilt her pleasure in her unexpected skill. It hurt and she didn't think she'd be able to carry anything for a while. She was glad to be swept off her feet so literally, if a little puzzled as to why.

Her new friend drove without speaking. Nina was glad, she was too tired for conversation. A reaction to the shock, she supposed. She leant her head against the headrest and closed her eyes. Pretty soon, she was asleep.

*

Marlene didn't notice that her passenger was asleep for quite a while. It was only when she realised she was hopelessly lost that she thought to check up on her silent companion. She stopped the car. Nina woke up.

She looked a bit startled.

'Where are we?' she asked.

'I don't know,' said Marlene. 'Can you see if there's a streetfinder in the glove box?'

Nina had a look. There was, but she couldn't see a street sign. They were in an industrial estate, which seemed to be completely deserted.

'I'll go and look,' Marlene said, glad to stretch her legs.

She couldn't get her shoes back on. She walked cautiously

to the nearest corner. There was a bridge going over a canal, and a telephone box, but no street sign. She crossed the bridge and opened the phone box door. She peered at the printed emergency instructions. Success.

Marlene was still too hot. She took off her jacket as she walked back to the car. She leaned in at the window and gave Nina the location.

Nina looked suddenly drained, and then excited.

'A phone box? Where?'

She leapt out of the car, and ran to the box. She dialled the number without checking it, suddenly confident that she had it lodged safely in her memory. She made her way back to the car, feeling so relieved she almost kissed Marlene. Instead she took the street finder from her, propped it on the bonnet and bent her head to the index.

'What was so urgent?' Marlene asked casually. Nina hesitated before answering.

'I was making an appointment to see a doctor about an abortion,' she said bluntly. She hardly knew Marlene, she didn't care what she thought. She turned her face down, pretending what she had said was mere small talk, and searched for the page, and then dissected the mass of streets, until she found Canal Row, corner of Lomax Street. She looked up, to find Marlene down to a baby-pink slip, under which she was fishing with great concentration.

'What are you doing?' she asked.

Marlene stopped struggling for long enough to explain.

'I'm trying to get my girdle off.'

Nina leant back and laughed. The girdle finally came loose and dropped about Marlene's ankles. She stepped out of it, kicked it away. She picked up her skirt, but it wouldn't go on without the girdle, that was why she bought the damn thing. She tossed the skirt and jacket into the back of the car. She looked at Nina, wonderingly. She knew what it cost to say things the way Nina said them, straight out. Throwing it in her teeth. She wished she had the courage to do the same. If she had that kind of courage she would say – I loved a woman once, loved her more than I should have, I think I could do it again, if –

Nina reached over and patted Marlene's stomach.

'You don't need a girdle, just clothes to fit,' she said. Her hand rested for a moment longer, with only the thin nylon slip between them.

Marlene couldn't breathe. The woman's hand was so warm and gentle and soft against her. It was anguish to just stand there, but Nina couldn't mean anything by it. Marlene wanted to lean into that touch, make something of it, but she didn't dare. She looked sideways at her companion, laying her hand carefully over Nina's. She forced herself to speak.

'So where are we?'

Nina withdrew her hand and gave her directions to get them back onto the ring road. She felt oddly rejected, she had wanted to go on sitting there, her hand trapped between Marlene's hand and her body. She had liked the feel of Marlene's body, gently rounded, generous, inviting in its warmth. But Marlene hadn't wanted her hand there. She was embarrassed, what had she been thinking of, why should she have wanted a total stranger touching her?

'Where do you want to go now?' Marlene asked, not at all sure Nina would get back into the car.

Nina looked at her, relieved. She had been expecting to be stranded on the industrial estate. She thought about going home, or going back to the supermarket to pick up the children. She wondered if they would still be there.

'Do you want to go home?' Marlene asked. Nina shook her head. Marlene looked down at herself.

'Wondering how to explain what you were doing in a

stolen car with a woman in her underwear?' she asked, wanting Nina to deny it.

'No, wondering how to explain why I left the children in the supermarket car park and ran away.' She hadn't even noticed that Marlene had said the car was stolen. Marlene thought about it. How many times had she wanted to just walk away and leave Abigail when she had been little? So many times she'd been a hair's breadth from it. She was still a little shocked. She searched for something to say that would sound as though she thought people left their kids in car parks every day.

'We could go and pick the children up. There's a party at my house later. My niece just got married. You want to bring your kids?'

Nina didn't really want to pick the children up, but none of it was their fault. Anything could have happened to them. She refused to think about it. She couldn't handle the idea of feeling guilty just now.

'And how are you going to explain turning up with a strange woman and her children in a stolen car?' Nina asked. So she had heard the bit about the car being stolen. She'd left out the underwear though, perhaps that was a good sign.

'I've done worse.'

'I bet you have,' Nina said, not believing that this respectable middle-aged woman could have had more than one strike for freedom. Marlene smiled, reading Nina's expression.

Think what you like, sugar, she thought. *You'll see.*

Marlene got the car moving as soon as she had got her breathing under control. Once they had turned a corner she could see the flyover. She knew where she was now. She drove steadily, singing along with Dinah Washington, up onto the slip road, and onto the ring road. The song changed and she couldn't sing anymore. Billie Holiday, *One More for the Road*? No, she'd crack up and cry, too emotional, she loved it.

Maybe ten minutes later, a police car appeared in her rear view mirror. She was feeling pretty good; she didn't need the police. She ignored them. She hadn't done anything. She was negotiating a difficult bend when the police car started its siren. It made her jump. Nina twisted round in the seat.

'They don't want us do they?'

'I'm afraid so,' Marlene said grimly. It was a difficult bend, it would be easy to crash. She thought about crashing the car, not having to answer the questions, face the embarrassment.

'So why aren't you stopping?' Nina asked, getting alarmed.

Marlene wondered why she wasn't stopping. Because she had stolen the car? Because she was dressed in nothing but her baby-pink slip? Because Nina was in the car? Because she was enjoying herself?

She kept driving. The police car swerved out and overtook, waving her down. She braked reluctantly, as they pulled in front.

'How are you going to explain this to your husband?' she asked Nina.

'I'll think of something,' Nina said. Marlene took her hand, as the policeman arrived at the car.

'It'll be all right,' she said.

'You bet,' Nina said, forcing cheerfulness into her voice.'You stick up for me, and I'll stick up for you.'

Marlene gave her a quick hug, grateful, relieved.

Nina liked the hug. She went on thinking how much she liked it as Marlene rolled the window the rest of the way down and leaned out to give the young policeman her best smile.

Nina laughed to herself, feeling reassured, confident. Somehow, Marlene would get them out of this. Perhaps she had done worse, she could certainly handle herself in a tight corner.

'Good afternoon, officer,' Marlene said calmly, 'How can I help you?'

BEHIND THE MASK

They say it started with a shepherd: a shepherd who handed an apple to a goddess; a goddess who had abandoned artifice and offered him a gift he could not resist; the most beautiful woman in the world.

And two slighted goddesses, who would normally have been indifferent to his opinion, took back their offered greatness, and in their own way undermined the gift of Aphrodite.

Hera, who had suffered many times from the infidelities of her husband, silently promised that he would indeed have the most beautiful woman in the world, but not to wife, for she was already married.

Athene, no lover of men, agreed he should have the woman, but she would bring him no love; bringing instead war and a terrible death as her dowry.

Aphrodite clasped the apple of discord to her breast and turned her eyes to seek out the prize for the shepherd who judged her greater than the Queen of Olympus.

And her eyes fell on the wife of Menelaus.

Athene laughed. Paris had made his choice, and must learn to live with his fate.

For Helen, it was different: she had not chosen.

When she raged against her fate, that was where she always finished. She had not chosen.

There had been many a suitor, many an eager king willing to wed a gawky untried girl for the benefit of her father's friendship.

She might have fared worse; Menelaus was, on the face of it, a fine specimen of a king.

Not yet old, strong, handsome in a rugged hard way, virile: Helen shuddered.

She had no say in the matter. She had sat silent and still while her fate was decided, a pawn to the politics of men. She had been old enough to understand, to be afraid, but not old enough to try the bounds of her father's affection, not old enough to say what she thought.

And so she had married, and left her home, with no one but a slave for company, to remind her that she had not always been the wife of Menelaus.

Her husband had done well out of the deal. To his surprise, his gawky little wife grew into a remarkably beautiful woman. Not that he waited to discover this before bedding her. He worshipped his virility and expected her to do the same, every night.

It was a relief to Helen to find she was pregnant, at least it gave her some hope of being left alone, if only for a while.

Shortly after her fifteenth birthday, Helen gave birth to her daughter. She had a hard labour, and for much of it she was convinced she would die, indeed, hoped that she would; but Helen did not die.

She could not bear the thought of being pregnant again, and the slave she had brought from her father's house found her potions to fool her body and keep Menelaus' seed from taking root.

For two years she endured his constant attentions, which were fired by her growing beauty and his determination to plant a son in her belly.

At last she gave in and stopped taking the drugs. She became pregnant almost at once, and again had a few short months' respite. This time the labour was easier and she brought forth a son.

Menelaus ordered a feast in her honour.

Helen found the noise and gaiety bewildering. She was

used to the quiet of the women's quarters, but now as the mother of his heir, she became a commodity that Menelaus wanted people to see. He paraded her; his pride and joy.

Helen found it as hard to live in the glare of his regard as she had done to live in the seclusion of her quarters.

She was his queen, sufficiently grown to take her place beside him at the head of the table, to serve his needs, to entertain his guests. She did all these things, but she did them the way a slave would, giving nothing of herself in the performance. She looked out at the world through a mask.

No one saw who she was, only what she was. Queen, wife, mother, beautiful. She had not realised that she was beautiful, but now every man in her husband's hall told her so. Beautiful, until she grew sick of the sound and wanted to disfigure herself so that they would stop. Helen looked with clear eyes from behind her mask, she looked at Menelaus, and hated him, hated him with such sudden sharpness, that not even the softness of his child's skin could dull the edge.

Menelaus was proud of his queen, proud of his good fortune. A young and obedient wife to bear his heirs, and the most beautiful woman in the world. His cup was full. Like all the others, he saw only the mask.

He was content with it. He did not ask who might be behind it.

Helen looked at her husband's guests and knew she should be grateful. She would not have wanted to be married to any of them; but all the time her despair and loneliness grew. She took no pleasure in her children, they served only as a reminder of the barren life that spread before her. It had no value to her, so she decided to end it.

The poison she took did not kill her, but it made her ill for a long time.

Menelaus came, talked to the doctor, patted her hand

and went away; just as he might check on an ailing horse. Once he knew that she was not going to die, he was not concerned.

Menelaus believed he loved his wife, but love for women was much the same as love for animals. He loved her for her beauty, her breeding, her skills. If she had died he would have been disappointed, but grief would have been short-lived, and quickly assuaged by the acquisition of a new wife.

Slowly, Helen regained her strength, and then the Trojan prince came.

Paris came: Paris, who had been promised the most beautiful woman in the world for his wife; Paris, who came as a guest to Menelaus' house, and left carrying away his host's wife: not her choice.

Helen was unused to being wooed, it alarmed her. She distrusted it and distrusted Paris; but he pressed his suit so insistently that she could scarce take breath, and it made a change. He was charming and gentle and at least seemed interested in her. He shook her out of her depression, like the creases being shaken out of a long stored length of cloth, so that she billowed and flowed in unexpected freedom of thought and sensation. But nothing Paris could do would still her restlessness; freedom of thought, yes, shackles fell from her mind in constant clamour, but where was her escape from her marriage, from her position, her beauty?

Menelaus never suspected for even a second that his quiet, obedient wife was, behind her mask, a whirlwind of confusion and possibility. Paris did not know what he was unleashing.

When the time came for Paris to leave, Helen regretted his imminent departure. It was as though, having opened the door to her cage, he was now closing it again, locking her back into her mask and silence. She did not know whether she could fold herself back into her submissive existence. It made her prison all the more unbearable, now that she had seen what she might be.

When it came to be time, Paris came to her and took her hand and he did not ask, *will you come with me*? He did not say, *will you leave this hall and be my wife*? He took her by the hand and said,

'You were promised to me by Aphrodite and you are coming with me.'

Helen struggled. Furious, not believing what he said, feeling tricked and betrayed. Seeing at last that the opening door had not been for her, but for him; that he would just lock her away somewhere different. Paris could not offer her the freedom she wanted. She called for help, but no one heard her, except Aphrodite, who knocked her senseless with an impatient flick of an eyelash.

No one heard but her slave, who watched and wept with impotence, too afraid of the prince and his armour and his sword to help her mistress. Weeping, because now she would be completely alone, and at the mercy of Menelaus' rage when he found his wife gone with the foreign prince. Then knowing suddenly what she must do, the slave picked the young son of Menelaus from his cradle and followed the man who carried the inert body of Helen down to the ships.

It was not Helen's choice to leave her husband and go to Troy with Paris. It was not her choice to take her son with her. As she had once been the pawn in the power games of kings, now she was a pawn in the games of the gods.

It was not her choice, but the situation had possibilities, and even advantages. For all Paris was an arrogant young rake, he did not take her for granted after that first struggle. A gift from the gods she might be, but he recognised that the gods had a warped sense of humour, that every gift has two sides, and sharp edges. He treated her with cautious respect and dignity, once he found that she was not a willing partner in his plans. He said nothing when he found her nursing her son, although he would have liked to throw the child into the sea to drown. He sensed that the two goddesses that he had angered were watching his every move, and would make his prize as difficult to keep as they could. But Paris had not guessed at half the trouble he had brought to his family with his choices, his judgement.

So Paris was cautious, generous, kind, even in bed, where there was another revelation. This vital young prince, herder of sheep, doom of his homeland, beloved of Aphrodite, was impotent. Had Helen felt less vulnerable in her precarious position, neither wife nor prisoner, she would have found it funny.

When they reached Troy, Helen discovered a new uncertainty, a new freedom. The Trojans did not know how to treat her. As Paris' wife, or his whore; as royal guest, or prisoner.

It was difficult for Helen to create a niche for herself in her new home, to adapt to the new way of living, but because the Trojans' expectations of her were so confused, she found she could be whoever she wanted to be.

Helen became herself for the first time. She did not allow Paris to lock her away again.

Freed of Menelaus' constant sexual demands, free of many demands from Paris, she began to explore in her mind what, if anything, she wanted from men. Gradually she learnt how to resist when she felt Aphrodite's guiding hand at the small of her back, impelling her towards Paris' bed. She refused to lie with him, impotent or not. It was a small victory, but it gave her the strength to take further control of her life.

When Menelaus launched his boats, it was not because he loved Helen. He did not care if she was beautiful or not, it was not because he needed her; he could get another wife.

Menelaus launched his ships because she was no longer

there. The injury to his pride was appalling. So damaging, that he almost shrugged her off rather than admit that she had run off with the foreigner; Menelaus valued his pride. But there was his son, also missing.

Menelaus was not an old man by the standards of his peers, but he was unlikely to father another legitimate heir. There was also the dynastic affair of Helen's dowry of islands and land rights.

Menelaus brought the wrath of the Argives down on Troy for his son, for his pride, but not for Helen.

And Helen, freed at last from the shackles of her mind, revelling in that freedom, managed to divorce the existence of her son from that of his father and allowed herself to love him. Loving her son fulfilled for her the total debt of love for men. She had grown to despise Paris. She loathed his touch and ignored him as much as she could, keeping to the women's quarters, discovering friendships with her new sisters, and the wives of her new brothers. She blossomed in the warmth of their kindness, and spent much time talking with her new family or walking the gardens or the city walls with only her slave for company. She was not entirely happy, but at least she could rest content.

Helen was on the wall when the first of her husband's ships was sighted on the horizon. She saw the red sails of the war fleet, watched the faint blur solidifying, growing, and understood the vast number of those ships. For barely a second she was flattered, but her slave, seeing the colour heighten in Helen's cheeks, spat at her feet. Startled Helen stared at her.

'Do not think he follows you out of love,' the slave said. She might have said more, but Helen needed no persuading. The brief flutter of pleasure that the sight of the fleet had instilled in her was gone, replaced now with a growing horror, a dread for what might come from this. She climbed down from the wall and went straight to the Temple of Aphrodite, begging her to avert the disaster that loomed now beyond the fertile plain of Illios. Aphrodite remembered Helen's rebellion, her resistance, and would not listen. Helen despaired. Hoping to find one friend still loyal to her now that she brought war to Troy, but knowing she might look in vain, she turned once more to her slave.

'Why did you follow me from the hall of Menelaus? Not from love, surely?'

The slave smiled, a little wistful at being asked so direct a question in such a way.

'I do not know what love is. I followed because your husband would have flayed me alive for not preventing your going.'

Helen smiled in her turn, feeling a certain kinship with her slave, she also did not yet know what love could be. Then her smile faded, and she wondered what her husband would do to her when he got her back. Menelaus, who did not love her; what welcome would she have from him, what might her fate be then?

Now the Trojans discovered what Helen was to be to them, neither prisoner nor guest. Now they saw her as a bringer of death and they hated her, blaming her, as they would not blame Paris who was their own, as she was not; the stranger in their midst. Even some of her new family, who after all knew how things stood between Helen and Paris, found it in them to turn their backs on her. Nothing was said, no one threw stones, threats or abuse, but their gazes followed her as she walked the city and that hatred burned her.

The Trojan warriors put on their bronze armour and went out to defend their city, to kill and to die, for the sake of a woman who wanted no part of their deaths.

The women of Troy turned back to their looms with

heavy hearts, wondering if the cloaks they now wove would be needed to shroud their menfolk. And in their hearts burned hatred for the Argives and their allies, but most of all for Helen, the cause of it all.

Helen: wife of Menelaus and the most beautiful woman in the known world. Pawn in the politics of men and the games of the gods. Helen who did not love her husband, nor Paris, nor any man.

Helen, who had not chosen.

PENELOPE IS NO LONGER WAITING

Penelope is no longer waiting. Her husband has been missing nearly ten years. Silently she agrees with the suitors who say he must surely be dead, secretly she hopes it is true, but knows that if anyone can take ten years coming home, if anyone can survive all the pitfalls of the anger of the goddess he has roused, he can. Publicly she denies his death and does not put on the mourning gown she made with her own hands these twelve years gone, in readiness.

Publicly she says that Odysseus will return to meet his nearly grown son, to claim his crown and to take back as his own his still beautiful wife.

Until then, her silence and the tilt of her head say: I rule here. As regent, certainly, but with pride and skill; and with a consort.

Daily she sits at her loom, weaving the beautiful, careful tale of her life.

Nightly, she rips it gleefully apart, each beautiful skilful lie.

Daily she rules with sense and courage the doubtful, restless people of Ithaca.

Nightly, she lies in the arms of her lover and wills her husband to the arms of the Siren, or the jaws of the Scilla, or the wiles of her sister Circe.

She thinks of how it will only be a few more years, and then her son will be old enough to rule. Then no one will want to marry her, and the endless stream of seemingly tireless suitors will fade away, leaving her to enjoy her retirement with the woman she loves. If only they can keep up the pretence those few years longer, if only Odysseus does not ever return.

Then, one day, a beggar comes to the door. Penelope looks him up and down suspiciously, she has been waiting for this. She recognises the ingratiating whine the man affects, she has heard it often enough before. She draws away from him, pretending disgust at his filth, straightens the crown on her noble brow. The blood pounds in her ears as she considers the puzzle before her. Her heart races with excitement and a little fear. She turns over the thought of poisoning the broth given him by the old woman who nursed him as a child. Knowing that she too will recognise him, she resists temptation.

She waits and watches as he slithers through her hall for a day and a night, sowing the seeds of discontent, setting one suitor on another, dripping his own subtle poison in each and every ear.

She sits motionless at her loom for hours, waiting, now, for a different moment. She reaches out a tentative hand and runs a finger along the dark thread she wove last, not yet ripped from the frame.

Odysseus will not be using this winding sheet after all.

She knows that soon he will declare himself, and she holds herself in readiness. On the second evening, she sees him rise to his feet, and she motions swiftly to the waiting servant. Odysseus straightens his back and cries aloud to the assembled throng that he is King of Ithaca, come home at last. A soft murmur of amusement runs through those dining at the Queen's table. He hesitates only a second, before holding up for all to see, a ring. Is this not the ring, with which Penelope encircled the finger of Odysseus when he went away to war? Indeed it is, but who but Penelope would recognise it after all these years?

She smiles to herself, a small, pitying smile, and stands.

Can this humble, ugly, dirty creature be her husband

returned? She asks those at her table. Would the great Odysseus creep into his own hall and not make himself known to his own wife for two whole days? Her voice shakes with anger. No, she says, he would not. Her husband, she cries, would sweep in with the night wind behind him, carrying the booty of his ten years journey and place it at her feet. This is nothing but a madman, a cruel charlatan, playing on the tolerance of their queen and she will have none of him, nor his tawdry ring. Then she orders him whipped from the city like so many previous pretenders to the crown she wears.

A paid assassin follows him, and later that night the ring he tried to give her as a token that he spoke truth is brought to her, stained with blood. She washes it tenderly, for her mother gave her that ring when she was married to Odysseus. When she goes to bed that night, she gives the ring to her lover to wear on her finger as a token of the love between them, that will never now be disturbed.

Penelope is no longer waiting.

REASON TO BELIEVE

Laura Templeton had, up until her thirty-seventh year, led what could be described as an uneventful life. When she stopped to think about it, her life had been remarkably peaceful until her marriage at the age of thirty-six. The marriage itself had almost taken her by surprise, and her husband's death, equally unexpected, within a year of their marriage, had changed her irrevocably.

Laura's attitude to life had not been precisely complaisant, more a cheerful and untroubled acquiescence with a fate that was mostly obliging in what it provided.

An only child brought up in comfortable, if mildly unconventional, surroundings, she had had a relatively untroubled progression from a girls' school in the south of England, to a reasonably distinguished degree at Oxford; this at a time when academic achievement in women was no longer a surprise, but was also no longer entirely fashionable.

Laura privately considered that her academic hopes had been restricted by her epilepsy, which caused her to lapse from consciousness for minutes at a time without anyone, herself included, noticing. This had an obvious disadvantage when studying, and more particularly, during exams. As a result, she had tended to compensate by being excessively thorough. Laura had therefore been part of a quiet and studious set. None of her chosen companions were real high flyers, so her obsession with working was accepted by them. They knew that the only way to secure a high-class degree was to work hard. This did not prevent them from leavening the serious study with long companionable walks, or visits to the theatre or cinema, and in this way Laura built up friendships she confidently expected to last for her lifetime.

Laura and her friends did well and found no difficulty in following their chosen careers. Laura took her history degree to a small but distinguished academic press and despite the fact that this was not entirely in line with her ambitions, lost herself to the work with equanimity.

When she analysed her attitude to work, she knew that she was doing more or less what she wanted, with a level of competence that both she and her employer found acceptable and she was therefore both happy and successful in a quiet way. This had resulted in her gradual progression to the most senior post within the company that would still provide a salary rather than a partnership.

The firm was a family concern, owned by Mr Stephen Webb who was, by the time of Laura's appointment to this senior post, a very old man. He had stayed on until his grandson Michael was old enough to take over, his son having been killed in an accident shortly after Michael's birth.

Laura was exceptionally fond of the old man, and, indeed, this fondness was returned, laced with professional respect on both sides. Over the years it had become a tradition for old Mr Webb to have lunch with his chief editor on a regular basis, and on occasion to invite the post holder to the opera, or some other form of respectable entertainment. With Laura's appointment to the post the entertainments and lunches increased their frequency and lost their formality; and Laura was wont to return to the office flushed with laughter and carrying small bunches of flowers. Mr Webb was a perfect gentleman and a generous employer. He made sure that working for Webb's was a pleasant experience.

*

Laura's private life was equally pleasant and undemanding. A small legacy from her grandmother had provided a comfortable one-bedroomed flat in a suburban area sufficiently far from town to be quiet, and blessed with an absence of motorways, but convenient for trains, which on a good day would get her to Waterloo in under forty-five minutes.

The flat itself was a conversion from a large house unsurpassed in its external ugliness, but well proportioned and spacious within. Having seen a few of the less fortunately converted, but prettier, properties local to her, Laura felt that she had made a successful move in securing this apparently unattractive home.

Her parents lived on the coast, in happy retirement. Elderly now, but fit and untroublesome. Indeed, never having been given cause to rebel against or even disagree with her parents, Laura's relations with them remained close and affectionate.

Laura was in the unusual position of being absolutely sure of herself, her surroundings and her beliefs. Not having been particularly troubled by either politics or religion, during her smooth transition from childhood to womanhood, she thought little of either.

Most political causes passed Laura by. She took no interest in either International or Home news. She had never experienced either discrimination or harassment on account of her gender, although she did realise that this was a fluke of good fortune. She rarely thought consciously of people as men and women, merely as friends, acquaintances, and people she did not know.

The impression Laura gave was that her life was happy and she needed nothing further to be fulfilled. In someone with an inquisitive and incisive mind this indifference to her surroundings might seem extraordinary, but the explanation was regrettably simple.

Her calm exterior was there to protect her. Her life was ruled by an undercurrent of disquiet, caused by the certainty that sooner or later her epilepsy would create a situation she would regret. She was withdrawn and reticent until she knew people well and avoided, as far as she could, situations where a sudden lapse of concentration could be disastrous; like climbing ladders, and romantic dalliance. She immersed herself in work, refusing to allow herself to get annoyed or flustered, in case it set off an attack.

One of the things missing from Laura's life as a result of her caution was, of course, sex. She might thrill to a well-turned courtly phrase in Middle French, which implied undying love, or even to the lasciviousness of John Donne; but it had never occurred to her that she needed or wanted a sexual partner. She would acknowledge that something was lacking from her life, but she did not think it was sex. What she hankered for was intimacy. But intimacy was not to be bought at the cost of her protective reserve. She was lonely, in a vague undefined way, when she bothered to think about it. Which is not to say that she never thought about herself in relation to sex, but these thoughts did not greatly disturb her. No one had ever raised her expectations or her blood pressure. Her own reserve had not encouraged any potential lovers to risk what they were sure would be a rebuff, and as a result she had reached the age of thirty-six a virgin.

Which had something to do with why she was so thrown by Michael Webb's proposal of marriage.

*

Michael Webb had spent his holidays from university working for the firm to familiarise himself with its operation, and had joined his grandfather's lunch parties. Falling into the habit, when the old man retired and handed over to his grandson, Michael continued to dine regularly with Laura, and to take her to the opera, or the theatre, becoming extremely fond of her in the process. Laura accepted his invitations happily; it had become so much a part of her life, almost a requirement of the job, that she thought nothing of it. Michael was good company, as his grandfather was, and she enjoyed being with him. The bunches of flowers were less discreet, the lunches more expensive, but she put this down to the exuberance of his extreme youth.

Michael was just turned twenty-five when his grandfather died. Stephen Webb was the first person Laura knew well to have died. (Her grandmother had lived in the Midlands and Laura had met her no more than once a year.)

It was a new experience for her, but not one that she treated as the painful reality it should have been. She rationalised her feelings. She consulted Donne. She asked for whom the bell tolled, and not liking the answer treated it as an historically specific response. She did not consider her own mortality, nor did she recognise that she was the loser, that her life was diminished by the loss of a dear friend. Not believing in an afterlife gave her neither comfort nor grief on behalf of her ex-employer. The life that had been Stephen Webb had ended, and that was that. The significance of that ending did not touch her, she turned her head away from grief as she did from anything that threatened her hard-won composure. Nonetheless, the grief was there and would catch her unawares.

Michael Webb, on the other hand, gave full vent to his feelings. He had loved his grandfather almost excessively and, although Stephen had been old, his death had been unexpected.

Michael became maudlin and unpredictable; and because neither his mother nor grandmother seemed capable of dealing with his grief, he turned to Laura for the comfort that she, too, was incapable of giving. Their lunches were replaced by what amounted to counselling sessions; Laura was out of her depth, confused by Michael's sudden emotional demands.

In some ways, her coolness and analytical approach calmed Michael. Laura viewed his distress with distaste rather than alarm and simply refused him enough space to wallow in his grief, afraid that, if she let him, she would be forced to examine or even explain her own feelings. Laura tried not to listen and found that often the only comfort she could give was to hold him, and say nothing. In this way they became used to touching one another, where, perhaps in other circumstances, they would have remained close but not intimate friends. They each found this gave them considerable pleasure.

Michael found himself depending on Laura. His gratitude for her kindness became confused with his growing affection. He needed her. She was the first woman who had stirred him to need. He felt he would always need her. It was almost a relief.

*

Laura attended the funeral for Stephen Webb. The office was closed for the day in any case, and all the staff were invited. Under any other circumstances, she would have stayed away, despite Stephen Webb having been her friend as well as her employer.

For the first time Laura met Mrs Webb - both of them. Mrs Webb senior, widow of the deceased, was shrunken and silent and dazed. Mrs Webb junior, Michael's mother, was officious and called everyone by their first name, whilst she would have been shocked to the marrow if Laura had dared to call her Jennifer.

Most of the authors also attended. Laura particularly noticed Philip Hansom. The only reason for this was that his latest work, *The Muse in Waiting – a treatise on the life and work of Anne Finch, Countess of Winchelsea,* was in her briefcase, awaiting her continued attention at the end of the funeral. A woman with him was introduced to Laura as his sister Alice. Had she been asked to describe her later, all Laura would have been able to say was that she had been wearing a black coat.

Alice Hansom would not, however, have been so vague

in her recollection of Laura, who was, despite her preoccupied and diffident air, a striking woman.

*

It was shortly after the funeral that Michael made his proposal. At first Laura thought she had misheard and asked him to repeat himself. This Michael did, looking faintly embarrassed.

Laura's first instinct was to ask why, which she subdued. Her second was to stall, and this she did with great firmness. She was shaken. She made an excuse to leave work early, an unheard of event. She phoned her mother from the station, and instead of returning to her comfortable flat, got on a train down to the coast and spent the night with her parents.

In turn, Michael was shaken by her response. He felt her panic to be infectious, and knew suddenly that he could not take no for an answer. He allowed her to put off answering his question with as much grace as he could drag from his limited reserve and spent an uncomfortable and anxious twenty four hours waiting for her response.

The Templeton family sat up late into the night. Laura was being forced to assess her life for the first time, to decide if she wanted to change it. She was also being forced to consider the necessity for carnal relations. She found herself unable to do so. Some deeply conventional part of her mind kept flashing dates at her; the number of years between Michael and herself: twelve in all. And then there was the epilepsy, about which Michael knew nothing.

Quite apart from anything else, Laura was not sure she believed in the concept of marriage. After all, her parents were not married, although their extreme respectability gave their neighbours the impression that they were. Laura's mother did attempt to suggest that living together temporarily might be a good idea, but Laura was not going to disturb her life for a temporary arrangement. Somewhere she had acquired and fossilised a belief in the permanence of relationships, and never having had one, had not been disabused.

Laura asked a great many questions, and was asked an equal number in return. Laura's parents neglected to ask one question, however. They did not ask whether Laura loved Michael, nor did Laura ask this question of herself.

*

The following morning Laura caught an early train and arrived at the office in time for nine o'clock. In her briefcase was a list of carefully phrased questions to which only Michael had the answers.

She felt uncomfortable, in creased clothes and uncertain frame of mind. She could not concentrate on her work and half way through the morning pulled out her list to add to it.

Catherine Exley, her assistant editor, noticed and asked what was wrong. Laura, looking distracted, merely asked her whether she had yet found herself somewhere to live. Catherine was taken aback at this; she did not realise that Laura had noticed her housing problem, it not being a result of land enclosure in the eighteenth century or whenever. She replied that she had not. Laura wrote *Catherine?* next to one of her questions and put her list away.

Lunchtime arrived, and Laura swept down the four narrow flights of stairs and out of the office. She crossed the road without looking and nearly ended her days beneath the wheels of a taxi.

She met Michael at their usual Thursday eating-place and put the first of her questions to him before she even sat down.

Was he sure he wanted to marry her?

His answer was adamantly affirmative, and he looked so worried and apprehensive that Laura abruptly and uncharacteristically forgave him for putting her in such a difficult position. She could not ask the rest of her questions, nor could she refuse him. She sat down, abandoned her list to her briefcase and caution to the winds: and said that she accepted his proposal. Michael's worried frown dissolved into a wide grin, which he hastily subdued, and he kissed her cautiously, formally, but tenderly on the mouth.

Laura returned to the office looking even more out of control than before. She enquired whether Catherine would be interested in visiting her flat with a view to renting it. Catherine would. She then made three phone calls.

The first was to her mother, to inform her of her decision. The second was to the register office to book the wedding. The third was to a lettings agency local to her home, to discover the going rate for one-bedroomed flats.

She then discussed terms with Catherine, which included a rent at two-thirds the sum she had been quoted by the lettings agency. Catherine agreed to visit the flat the following day after work.

Laura then phoned Michael; to inform him that she had arranged the wedding for a Friday three weeks away, and that in all probability Catherine would take over her flat the following Monday, giving them the weekend to move her belongings out. Which showed that Laura was not unworldly when she put her mind to it.

*

Laura visited Michael's home for the first time. To say that she had not known what to expect would be theoretically correct, but would not do justice to her powers of deduction. Having been jolted out of her usual indifference, Laura had imagined every variation on the bachelor flat of a twenty-five-year-old with money, and her imagination had included a fair approximation of the reality.

Michael had not developed any particular taste, so he bought someone else's. His rooms were exquisitely and expensively decorated and furnished by a firm of up-and-coming interior designers, one of whom he had shared rooms with at Cambridge for a time, before his friend had thought better of academia and left for art school. As a result, to the casual observer, nothing was revealed of Michael beyond his broad tastes in architectural design.

Closer observation would pinpoint the few objects which were Michael's own choice – the books, a lump of unworked amber, the litter of papers falling out of an over-stuffed desk. Having committed herself, Laura felt the need to discover what she had let herself in for. Armed with a stiff gin, which she would not normally have allowed herself, she investigated Michael's home thoroughly. Michael lounged in various doorways watching. He had retired to the sofa and a second gin by the time she started her run of the books.

Many of them were their own publications. There were a great many poetry books, the earliest of which seemed to be Walt Whitman. Laura began to wonder how compatible they were going to be. The novels were even less promising. She recognised only a scattering of authors, and the titles did not spark her interest.

Laura gave up and joined Michael on the sofa. Her gin was replenished.

She and Michael discussed many of the topics that had been on her list in a considerably more tactful and roundabout way than she had planned. A warm glow suffused her, reminiscent of comfortable evenings spent with her friends at college; she decided it was going to be all right after all. They discussed who to invite to the wedding.

Rather shyly, Michael read Laura a poem he had written for her. Laura discovered to her surprise that he was really quite good at it. She also realised that she was happy, and that Michael really did feel quite intensely about her, while she did not feel the same about him. This made her feel guilty and the small amount of alcohol, which she was not used to, encouraged her to do something to expiate her guilt. So she leant over and kissed him. The kiss lingered, and fired, and she found herself being embraced. The kiss became passionate and, to her enormous relief, arousing; one thing led to another until Michael led her to bed.

Laura was surprised how much she enjoyed Michael's lovemaking, especially as she had been afraid that she would not find it enjoyable in the least. Although, in her usual analytical way, she admitted to herself that actual intercourse was rather dull by comparison to the other things they did. For his part, Michael was surprised that she was a virgin. It hadn't occurred to him; he was rather pleased.

*

Having overcome this major and daunting hurdle, the weeks flew past and the wedding was upon them.

Laura did not enjoy being the centre of attention. She felt vulnerable in her new state as an attached woman; she did not know how to behave. Had she read more contemporary fiction, she might have picked up some useful pointers, but she had not. Her wedding guests, Marjorie, Caroline and Shirley, her friends from college, were no assistance, never having taken the plunge themselves. They were surprised, even disappointed, at Laura's turning renegade on them.

The ceremony was a civilised affair, followed by an uncomfortable gathering in a hotel, where the sparsity of guests became apparent. Laura was glad that custom allowed the bridal pair to leave first, and looked forward to it.

It was at the reception that she met Philip Hansom's sister again. In her new state of heightened awareness, Laura took more notice and observed her willowy grace and her remarkable features with something approaching jealousy. However, she swallowed her gall and made conversation. She found herself captivated. Alice said little, but what she said was to the point. Among her few observations on Laura's new career as a wife, she suggested that Laura and Michael should not spend their honeymoon shifting furniture. Laura had forgotten about the peculiar tradition of taking a holiday to get to know your spouse.

That night, she and Michael lay together in the same bed for only the second time, and Laura reflected that a period of adjustment would have been a good idea. After all, she hardly knew Michael. She shivered, feeling cold without her nightdress, and Michael, misinterpreting this as a shudder of desire, renewed his impassioned exploration of her body. Laura liked the feel of his warm hands sliding over her cold skin, it was comforting. But tonight she was not drunk and the disconnectedness of their previous encounter would not rescue her from either the cold or her whirring brain.

She clung, pressing herself against him to keep warm; but she found his body unyielding, hard with muscles and passion. She wanted to talk to him, but he was off in a world of his own, a physical world full of sensations he fondly imagined she was sharing.

Laura decided she was angry, and that this was no way to start conjugal life. She didn't want him. Not now, not like this, sweating and gasping and heaving over her, while she lay there with a headache growing.

Laura thought about building a wall: it was made of beautiful stone, glinting with agate fire, cold and hard and slippery. Each block weighed a great deal and as she lifted them, placed them so precisely, all the muscles in her body tensed against the weight.

She became aware that Michael was no longer lying over her, and that she was cold again. She pulled the bedclothes around her, and stared at her husband's face. He looked so young and vulnerable. She wanted him to be happy. She wanted him to make her happy. She wanted to be able to respond to his lovemaking. She wanted to cry.

Michael reached out and pulled her close to him, stroking the hair away from her face.

'You passed out,' he said quietly.

Laura buried her face in his shoulder. Hadn't she always known? Thank god she had never yet had a major fit, just this slipping in and out of consciousness. And she still hadn't told him.

Laura might not have told Michael about her epilepsy, but her mother, sensible woman, had.

Michael fished in the bedside cabinet for the book on epilepsy that he had borrowed from the library. He tapped Laura on the shoulder with it.

Laura burst into tears.

*

They spent the weekend moving Laura's belongings from her flat. Although she had not acknowledged it, Laura was looking on this as a temporary move, which was why Catherine was renting the flat. They also spent the time talking – about themselves, about each other, about sex. Laura tried to explain what went wrong the previous night, about building the wall in her head, about not being able to let go. Michael tried to understand. They ended up joking about leaving the heating on at night, and resolved nothing.

Laura did not say that she found penetration boring, verging on distasteful; and Michael did not tell her that he had only the haziest idea of what made sex good for a woman. Nor did he tell her the main cause of his ignorance. Instead he resolved to buy a book on the subject. Despite this resolve, he did not purchase any such volume, being too embarrassed to do so. In any case, he felt sure that they were suffering from the usual difficulties in adjustment that any newly married couple might experience and expected matters to sort themselves out. Perhaps it was more than an assumption; he was determined that it would be so; expecting Laura to make all the necessary adjustments. Laura was not the sort of woman to make these sort of changes.

*

After a month or so they had settled into a routine of life that, apart from sexually, was satisfactory to both. In bed, Michael found himself losing interest and whilst their lovemaking continued tender, it was less passionate and less frequent. Laura was relieved at this. They spent their evenings listening to music, reading, and talking in a comfortable and desultory fashion. The occasional visit to their respective parents, and the continuance of their excursions to the theatre served for social life.

Philip Hansom was a regular visitor, but even though she knew far more about Philip's field of research than her husband, Laura felt excluded from the conversation when he and Michael talked. Whenever she made an observation, there would be an almost imperceptible silence as though the men were adjusting to accommodate her. Laura felt that she was being patronised, not a feeling she was used to. On return visits, Alice would occasionally join them. Then they listened to what Laura had to say; it was as though Alice provided a bridge, or simultaneous translation. Laura grew to be very fond of Alice, who was a witty raconteuse, and whose slow, lazy way of speaking almost hypnotised her.

After a while, the two women forged an independent relationship and saw each other without the men present. This time became precious to Laura, but she was never confident that Alice felt equally enthusiastic.

*

Often, when Michael visited Philip, Laura would visit Alice. She was fascinated by Alice's house, which was beautiful, and sufficiently old to interest the historian in Laura.

Alice was comfortably rich and did not work, feeling she should leave the jobs for those who needed them. In her youth she had been extremely wild, much to Philip's embarrassment. He did not share her good fortune in her inheritance, nor her taste in activities or friends, most of whom he considered dangerous and vicious. She had, however, calmed with the onset of her thirties, having learnt the hard way that Philip was right about at least some of her so-called friends. She now had few friends of her own, was fond of her own company, and liked to share some of Philip's friends. But Laura was a different matter. She felt as though Laura had been a missing part of her life, which was now made whole.

Summer came, and Alice reminded Laura of her long delayed honeymoon. She suggested that Laura and Michael join Philip and herself on their holiday. They had hired a farmhouse in the Lake District for a month, and they would welcome company for all or part of the time. Laura was delighted, and touched. When she broached the idea with Michael he laughed and said that Philip had also suggested that they join forces for their holiday.

*

It was about this time that Laura received a profound shock, one that rocked the foundations of her existence.

Waiting in the living room at Alice's house while Alice changed into a cooler dress after work, she idled her way through the bookshelves, and picked out a book almost at random. She could not afterwards say why this book had drawn her attention. She opened it to read the flyleaf, and was confronted by her husband's handwriting. A short verse proclaimed undying sexual passion. Laura's lungs clenched. She could not focus her eyes. She struggled for a while to calm herself. When she could bear to, she looked again and re-read the verse. This time she realised that it was not, as she had first assumed, addressed to Alice. It was addressed to her brother.

When Alice returned to the living room, Laura was chewing her lip, and pulling at the neck of her dress, the book dangling limply from her hand. Alice realised at once that something was very wrong and took the book from Laura's hand. She glanced at it and put it back on the shelf.

Laura surfaced again. Alice told her that she had just had a fit, and asked what had set it off. Laura looked for the book. Alice had hoped that it would have been conveniently wiped from Laura's memory by the fit, but this was not to be. She retrieved it from the bookshelf, now fervently wishing she hadn't borrowed Mary Renault's *The Persian Boy* from Philip.

Alice put her arms about her friend. She tried to explain that her brother and Michael had indeed been lovers, but this was no longer the case, and hadn't been for some time. Laura extricated herself from Alice's embrace. She didn't know what to believe, she didn't even know what to think. She went home.

Michael was pleasantly surprised to see her. He hadn't expected her to be home until late. Laura was distant with him, not able to bring herself to speak much, unable to tell him what she had discovered.

That night in bed, Michael began stroking her back as a prelude to more passionate dalliance. Laura froze, and as his hand moved down over her shoulder towards her breast, she pushed him away and sat up. She told him then that she knew of his relationship with Philip. Then she cried. She was furious with herself, she had hoped to be rational and dignified, but was unable to stop and gasped out her recriminations in an incoherent fashion between sobs and bouts of torrential weeping. All her disappointment in their sex life was poured into her vilification of her husband's deceit. For the moment she could see no further than this betrayal of trust.

Michael did not attempt to shout over her weeping. He

waited until she had exhausted herself, and then he gathered her, unresisting, against his chest and told her of his affair with Philip. How it had started when he was working at the firm during the college holidays, of the intensity of his emotions for the older man, of their long correspondence during term time, how they had renewed their relationship each holiday, of his gratitude to a tender and loving sexual partner.

He told her how they had drifted apart as he grew older, became more experienced in the ways of the world, began treating their relationship as a problem rather than a pleasure. He told her of Philip's eventual leave taking, telling him that he had obviously outgrown the relationship, but that he hoped they could remain close friends. And they had. He told her that he had not slept with Philip for over a year before they had married, that he had never had any other male lovers, and, for good measure, that he had had an AIDS test before he proposed to her. In conclusion he said that she had nothing to fear from his relationship with Philip, past, present or future.

Laura wanted to believe him, but she could not see how all this answered her basic complaint of dishonesty; it also sounded rehearsed. But she was too tired to protest further, even when Michael's hands began to trace patterns on her body again. She lay against him, too exhausted to move, past caring what he did. She found herself drifting half into sleep. In her dream she was searching a huge supermarket for onions and, no matter where she looked, she could find none. At last she tracked down the vegetable department, but there was a huge scrum of people around the onions. She pushed her way through, and was just reaching out to pick one up, when Michael orgasmed with great gusting groans, and woke her up. It was most frustrating. She fell asleep again almost immediately, trying to puzzle out what onions had to do with anything.

*

After this there was a coolness in relations between the Webbs and the Hansoms. Indeed there was a coolness between Laura and Michael. She was less willing to tell him her intimate thoughts, and was suspicious of any time he spent away from her, especially if she knew he was with Philip. But gradually, as there was no sign of anything between the two men that could conceivably cause her anxiety, the old regime was reinstated. So when the subject was again broached, she was willing to carry out their original plan to join Alice and Philip for the last two weeks of their holiday.

They travelled by train and were met by Alice at the station. The weather had been unusually fine, so that Alice's normally dull hair was bleaching to a subtle gold and her skin was darkening to match. She kissed them both in a very relaxed fashion, flinging their suitcases casually into the back of Philip's battered Volkswagen. When they'd climbed into this ancient vehicle, Alice drove them at a reckless pace through the town and along a steadily ascending road through two villages before turning into a sharp bend that took them onto a farm track. Laura was thrown against Alice by the sudden veering of the car and had some trouble extricating herself.

The house was a solid, low built farmhouse with dormer windows that glowered out from the roof towards magnificent scenery. The back of the house caught the afternoon sun and faced a small spinney beyond which lay a tarn. Laura followed Alice up to their room, which faced over the courtyard to the rear. It was furnished with a vast, deep and very soft double bed, a bow-fronted chest of drawers and a cavernous wardrobe. Next to it was a distinctly spartan bathroom. Alice had the bedroom opposite and Philip was in the room next to hers, opposite the bathroom.

Michael struggled up the stairs with their suitcases, and Alice left them to unpack, saying that when they had finished they should come down to the tarn and swim. Laura and Michael faced each other over the bed, glad the journey was over, anticipating a fortnight's idleness.

The weather was kind to them, lapping them in balmy sunshine and warmth. Laura felt as though she were caught in some dream of perfection, and that she would wake up to discover that the outside world had moved on a century overnight. She could not remember finding it so easy to be happy; each day was filled with laughter, exploration, talk, gentle exercise, and love.

She supposed that this was how a honeymoon should be, but she knew that had she been alone with Michael, it would not have been the same, would not have been idyllic. She even found herself enjoying Philip's company. But it was Alice who filled her waking hours, and some of her sleeping ones as well.

Several days into their stay Laura woke, or dreamt she woke, in the middle of the night to find Alice standing beside her. The semi-light from the window behind her put Alice's face in shadow. Laura stared up at her, trying to see her features, but it was impossible. Alice stretched herself out beside Laura, her skin dark against the white of the coverlet. She reached out a hand to smooth Laura's hair. Then her hand trailed down Laura's neck, and into her nightdress.

Laura decided she must be dreaming, not because Alice was undoing her buttons, but because she was lying beside her in bed, where Michael should be; and if Michael was not there, she must be dreaming. She put her hand next to Alice's face, not quite daring to touch, because she would not be able to feel her, if she was dreaming. She could hardly credit that she would dare to dream this. Alice turned her head and first her lips and then her teeth grazed the tips of Laura's fingers. Laura shuddered.

Alice's lips caressed the inside of her wrist and Laura sighed, and thought what a pity it was that it wasn't possible;

and because it was a dream, Alice asked her why it wasn't. And Laura told her that she was such a good friend, and that she loved her so much, that an affair was out of the question; but even as she said it her body was responding to Alice's touch and her own hands were stroking Alice's breasts.

Again Alice asked her why. It took some time for Laura to get her mind round the reasons, she found it difficult to concentrate against the growing sensations of warmth and fluidity that coursed through her limbs.

'Because affairs are only temporary, and I want you for ever and ever,' she said hopefully.

And because it was a dream Alice wasn't shocked or scornful, and she laughed, and said, 'We could easily make love for ever and ever.'

But Laura was a rational person, and even in a dream her rationality asserted itself, and she said,

'No, I am married to Michael, and that is the only thing that is forever.'

And the dream ended.

*

The next morning, Laura slept late. When she woke, the bed beside her was empty. She struggled out of the tangle of bedclothes, finding this difficult because her nightdress was undone and tangled around her arms in a most inconvenient fashion. She felt unrested and frowsty. She suddenly remembered her dream, and blushed. She got up and dressed in her swimming costume, grabbed a towel from the rail in the bathroom, found her sandals and walked briskly down the stairs. The house was silent and empty. There was coffee on the hotplate in the kitchen, and bread cut ready. She pushed open the kitchen door and stepped from the coolness into the sunlight. The heat made her feel better, and she shrugged off the feeling of irritation, and relaxed. Everyone must be at the tarn already.

Laura walked slowly through the trees beside the tarn enjoying the early sun and listening to the laughter of the bathers she could not yet see. Then she came out of the trees and saw Alice sitting silently beside the water smoking a cigarette. Which meant that the two men splashing about in the shallow water were responsible for all the noise. Laura sat down beside Alice, who turned her green-hazel eyes on her and smiled the smile that turned her stomach to molten fire. Laura smiled back and her heart beat faster, so that she had to look away. The heat of the day was already making steam rise from the lake.

She tried to concentrate on the horseplay of the men, she tried to pretend she didn't mind when she saw them embrace. But she could not see their kiss as innocent, it went on for too long. She rose to her feet abruptly, and ran back to the house.

She was pouring coffee when Alice came into the cool darkness of the kitchen. Her hand slid along Laura's bare arm and Laura put her own hand to cover it, meaning to push her away, but instead they stood completely still, hands touching.

Laura struggled to speak, finally saying;

'He told me it was finished. He said he loves me.'

Alice sighed, and disengaged her hand to push the hair out of her eyes.

'He does love you. But it just isn't that simple. He's known Philip a long time, and loved him a long time. He can't just write him off.'

'But he doesn't have to kiss him.'

'Why not? I kiss you.'

'That's different.' Laura said, knowing as she said it that it was not different.

'Why did he marry me?' she cried, despairing. Asking more than one question. Why *him*? Why *me*? Why *married*?

Alice took the coffeepot from Laura and put it down firmly.

'He couldn't very well marry Philip, could he?' she asked,

angrily. Laura stared at her in surprise and caught the look of remorse that crossed Alice's face and, as quickly, gave up wondering why Alice was trying to hurt her.

She remembered her dream, remembered thinking that only her marriage had substance, and here she was faced with a blunt truth. If he had been given a fair and equal choice between Philip and herself, despite every assurance he had given, Michael would not have chosen her. She had been lied to and tricked.

She stared at Alice, remembering her hands, her lips exploring her body. She wondered whether she had any right to criticise Michael. But then, that had only been a dream. She turned her back on Alice and drank her coffee.

Laura spent the whole day in a turmoil of emotions. She could not settle to anything or make civil conversation. Instead she went for a long walk on her own, and spent some time crying. She did not feel that she could trust anyone, least of all Michael. She wondered whether the invitation to stay had been purely to give Philip time with her husband, and whether Michael had been party to the scheme, or had been seduced for the second time on their arrival. And had Alice been brought along to keep her occupied? She could scarcely bear to think it.

That night her thoughts kept her silently and rigidly awake, and when Michael slid from their bed and vanished for three hours, she lay crying weakly, until she exhausted herself and slept.

Philip did not cry himself to sleep. He welcomed Michael into his bed with surprise, and pleasure. They had kissed, certainly, but he had not thought to expect this. It was almost painful, wrenching his attitudes back to treating Michael as a lover. He was not sure he wanted to. It was a long time since their last, he had thought their final, goodbye. And now here was Michael creeping into his bed, leaving his wife of only a few months. It was cruel, Philip thought. Cruel to Laura, cruel to him. But all the same, risks aside, potential pain aside, here was a man he loved, close and amorous. Philip would face the consequences when they bit, not go looking for them. When Michael lay asleep in his arms, he rested his chin gently on the top of his lover's head and regretted it. There could be no going back now, he could not rebuild his careful indifference; but now there was Laura to get in the way, to get hurt. Michael would have to make a choice.

When Laura woke it was late morning and pouring with rain. Michael lay beside her, an expression of angelic serenity on his sleeping face. To prevent herself from slapping him, she got up and ran a hot bath. Usually the long soak would have restored her spirits, but this time it failed dismally and she returned to the bedroom resolved to do battle. Michael had eluded her, however, and had gone downstairs. She dressed quickly, meaning to confront him over the cornflakes, before Alice and Philip joined them. She did not want an audience. But she was too late. They ate breakfast in silence, her fury impressing itself on them all.

Because of the rain, and because of the frosty atmosphere, Alice spent the morning searching through various tourist leaflets she had found in the sideboard, and making suggestions as to places of interest they might visit to while away the afternoon. They eventually agreed on a National Trust property that was, when she looked at the map, some distance away. However, they found their waterproofs and crowded into the car. Alice drove, Philip beside her reading the map. Laura sat stiffly beside Michael, trying not to touch him when a bend in the road sent her sliding against him on the slippery vinyl seat.

Alice put on the radio to cover the tense silence that was only broken by Philip's murmured directions.

The house was disappointing. They trailed dutifully and politely round the staterooms, then gratefully discovered the gardens, and the sun that had broken through the cloud cover and already dried all but the most resistant puddle.

They strolled slowly around the gardens, Philip and Michael relaxed and casual with one another, Alice and Laura at arms length, not speaking. Half way along the gravelled terrace, Alice noticed that her brother was attracting the attention of a couple of women. She smiled to herself, thinking that they were comparing notes on his attractiveness. She was really quite proud of her brother. As she drew closer, one of the women looked in her direction, then whispered to her companion. They both smiled benevolently at her. There was something strange about it. Alice took a moment to realise that the smile had encompassed Laura as well as herself, and was one of recognition. Her answering smile froze into stiffness. She hoped Laura had not noticed. She glanced again at her brother and Michael, heads bent together over some plant, hands not quite touching.

She turned to look at the two women as they passed her, caught them smiling together at their secret understanding and a sudden wave of longing caught her. She wanted what they had, what Philip had. She wanted to be recognised by the company she kept. She only wished that what they thought about Laura and herself were true. She looked at Laura, trapped in her misery, and thought about permanence and marriage, and love and – Anna. Her mind twisted away desperately, not wanting to remember the last time she had felt like that, wanting that sort of recognition, wanting that sort of love. She switched her brain off firmly. She threaded her arm through Laura's in a casual, friendly way and kissed her lightly on the cheek. She had kissed her friend this way many times before but this time Laura's cheek reddened, and she could see the pulse quicken in the vein in her neck. Alice wondered if she was going to regret that impulsive kiss, but Laura said nothing, and some of the tightness went out of her shoulders. All the same, Alice let her hand drop in as casual a way as she could manage.

On the drive home she sat in the back with Laura and Michael drove. She cherished every bend in the road that left her no choice but to lean against Laura.

That night Alice lay awake, and heard the door of Laura and Michael's room open and close in the early hours of the morning. She held her breath, thinking of Laura, but the footstep went to Philip's door, and the door opened, and closed, and did not open again until she was asleep.

*

This time, Philip could not decide if he was glad of Michael's company. Of course he wanted him, but like this? Sneaking about in the dark? And for how long? How soon would it be before he went back to his safe, unpushy wife. He asked Michael this. A mistake. He dealt with the resulting torrent of promises as though he believed them. He did not. He knew Michael too well.

When Michael got out of his bed in the early hours of the morning, Philip was angry, really angry. Going back to his wife, going to lie with her, to lie to her. As he had been lied to. It was impossible. He said so.

Michael stared out of the window at the rain, still falling in sheets, not wanting a row. Not wanting to hurt Philip, or be hurt. Not wanting Philip, or Laura, or anything much. He felt exhausted. He knew that Philip did not trust him, that Laura did not trust him. He loved them both; differently, but equally. Philip's snort of derision when he had told him this had been hurtful, but he had understood it. He had a choice to make and he did not want to make it. He sat down again on the bed. He put his arms around Philip and hugged him close, tight. And then he left him.

*

When Laura woke she was alone. A moment's anxiety

was immediately allayed by the sound of running water in the bathroom. Michael had returned from his nightly tryst and was showering. It was only when the shower finished that she realised the tune Michael had been whistling was uncharacteristically out of period, being at least seventeenth century if not earlier. Indeed, she surmised that it was not Michael at all. It was Philip. She looked at her watch. It was quite late. Perhaps Michael was already breakfasting. The smell of coffee was noticeably absent. She heard Philip's whistling receding to his bedroom, and then the bathroom door shut again. The shower resumed. Laura was angry. He hadn't even bothered returning to her bed. This blatant breach of manners could only mean that he had decided to leave her. They hadn't even spoken of the situation. Was this supposed to be her first intimation, his not returning to bed? She leapt out of bed, and stormed out of the bedroom, knocking loudly on the bathroom door. Finally, the door opened, to reveal Alice, hastily and inadequately wrapped in a towel, Laura was speechless. Could Michael still be in Philip's bed? Leaving Alice staring at her she threw open the door to Philip's bedroom. Philip was alone. The fact that he was half dressed in a suit reminded her that it was Sunday, and that Alice and Philip were preparing to go to church.

'Where is my husband?' she demanded, through gritted teeth. The look of puzzled dismay on Philip's face only infuriated her.

'I know he was with you last night. He hasn't come back to bed, where is he?'

Philip now looked alarmed.

'Are you sure?' he asked, 'He left me three hours ago.'

Laura did not know whether to be concerned as to Michael's disappearance or outraged at Philip's brazen admission.

'Then you had better find him,' she shouted, 'before you go to confession.'

She stormed back into her bedroom, and threw herself

on the bed, too angry and alarmed to cry.

Alice joined her, a tentative hand stretched out to stroke her back and then withdrawn. Laura made an effort to turn over. She knew she was over-reacting, that probably Michael was simply swimming in the tarn again. The trouble was that she could no longer contain the anger and misery and needed to shout and scream and make a scene.

Alice sat beside her on the bed, holding her hands gently. She had to admit that Michael had treated Laura appallingly and that Philip had richly deserved to be bawled at. Laura tried to smile at her; and Alice found herself longing to hold her, really hold her, close, face to face, breast to breast, flesh to flesh.

Laura looked across at Alice, struggling to banish the thought that was pounding through her veins; the thought that wanted to reach up and pull Alice against her, and kiss her in a quite different way from that gentle brush of the lips which had stirred her blood the day before.

She pulled very gently at Alice's hands, and found her responding with a swiftness and ease she could scarcely credit. She let go of Alice's hands and wrapped her arms about her, pulling her close, pulling her down to lie beside her. It was different from the dream. Far more urgent and passionate, more physical. Wave after wave of desire sent her reeling, scarcely conscious of what she was doing, wanting only to touch and be touched, to kiss and be kissed in a frenzy of insistence, and a whirlpool of delight that all her wanting was echoed two, three times over. And that was only the first kiss. Laura was dizzy for lack of air, they had to stop, take breath, examine their motives; but Alice would not let her, and soon she stopped trying to think, and concentrated on the matter in hand, the matter in tongue.

She forgot all about her missing husband.

Philip, in an uncharacteristic show of independence, did not go looking for Michael, and did not wait for his sister. He did not want to be late for church.

So it was not until he was walking back from the village that he went to look at the tarn. He was hot, the weather was too warm for suits, and the suit he wore was not of the coolest fabric possible. He was thinking about swimming and scanned the water almost casually. Then his eye caught the white glint of something floating in the water. At first he thought it was a dead swan, having seen one on more than one occasion. But on each of those occasions there had been a live swan on guard over the body of its mate. He looked, but did not see it. A strange foreboding slid into his heart and he began running along the path. The dread became horrified certainty and he did not stop as he reached the water's edge, flinging himself into the water, wading out as fast as the resistance, and the sudden unexpected coldness of the water would allow.

Up in the house, Alice heard the cry of anguish and trembled. Laura heard it, and felt the blood drain into her heart and then burst at speed back into her veins; her hands shook. They looked at each other across the kitchen table, then, without speaking, ran out of the kitchen door and across the courtyard.

Laura's heart pounded, her feet skidded on the grass. Her breath came in short gasps. Over and over she said to herself, *it can't be true, this isn't happening*. But it was true, it was happening. Philip was drowning her husband in the tarn. The world fell away from her, and she stopped running.

Laura stood staring at the water, blankly, twisting her hands together. She made herself stop twisting her hands, made herself move forward, away from the trees.

By the time she reached him, Philip had pulled Michael from the water and was trying to force the liquid out of his lungs. Alice had taken one look, and turned back, running to the house, to the phone. Laura limped to a stop, hardly daring to look at her husband.

Of course he was dead. His slim, pale blond body was dragged from the weeds quite naked, quite lifeless. She stared at the muddy streaks of water on his back and thought that he did not look human, did not look as though he had ever been alive. Like an unfinished clay model, its shape beginning to dissolve in the water. She felt as though she, too, was dissolving, and stood rooted to the spot. Time passed. She did not know how many minutes she had stood without moving. Suddenly, reality reimposed itself. She looked at the scene before her as if for the first time, and was not sure how she had got there. Philip turned Michael over and started blowing air into his lungs. Two breaths. He placed his fingers against the artery in the limp neck. His eyes drifted to Laura.

'Can you do this?' he asked. She nodded wordlessly, glad to have someone tell her what to do, what to think. She knelt beside her husband and blew air into his lungs while her husband's lover knelt besides her pushing down on Michael's chest. The first few minutes before they could check the pulse again seemed like an hour, the time it took for the ambulance to arrive was a century. They worked steadily together, two breaths, five compressions, and never a hint of life.

When the ambulance and the doctor and the police arrived, and crowded her out, she allowed Alice to lift her up, to turn her about and lead her away. Her steps were uncertain, her mind filled with the muddy water streaming from his yellow hair.

She could not understand how he had come to drown. He was a strong swimmer. The water wasn't even deep. A terrible doubt began to grow in her mind. She could remember nothing since she woke until she came running down the grassy slope to find Philip hauling Michael's limp body from the water. What had happened? Why was Michael lying there in the water, still and cold?

She drank the hot sweet tea Alice thrust into her

hands without tasting it. She saw, without registering it, the ambulance take her husband away. She remembered watching him walk down the path away from the house, a towel over his shoulder. Her memory faltered. She had not seen him this morning. Why was it only this time that Philip had not gone swimming too?

She watched Philip walk through the kitchen, wet to the armpits, his clothes dripping water onto the floor, like tears. He shrugged off Alice's restraining hand and slammed the door behind him. Even though the walls of the house were thick, she could hear him crying in his bedroom. She did not really believe that he could have drowned Michael, did she?

Alice sat at the other side of the table from her. Laura noticed that the ends of her hair were wet. She reached out to touch. Wet. Alice's hazel eyes flickered from her hand to her face.

'You should rest.'

'I've done with sleeping,' Laura replied, not knowing what she meant.

Alice frowned.

'You can't keep going for ever,' she said.

'Nothing is for ever,' Laura said, and wondered if she had really been asleep that time, when Alice had come to her room – Alice blinked. Laura's hands began to shake. She knit her fingers together round the mug of tea, and took a gulp of air. She knew it was crazy, what she was thinking. Why should Alice want to hurt Michael? She ran a hand through her hair, it was wet.

Perhaps *she* had drowned Michael. The whole thing was ludicrous, but why couldn't she remember what had happened this morning? She must have had a fit, and now she couldn't remember what had happened. It had never been this bad before, she had never lost more than a few minutes, at least as far as she had been able to tell. Why now, when it was so important to remember, had she lost a whole morning, a whole night?

Laura felt her grip loosening, couldn't feel the cup in her hand. She tried to stand up and found her sight greying and her ears buzzing.

'I'm going to faint,' she said, and did.

*

She woke with a crowd of people in the room, Alice, two members of the police, and the doctor. The doctor was talking about shock, Alice about epilepsy. The police were exchanging notes. She wanted them all to go away. She struggled upright on the sofa, and they all made expressions of satisfaction. Alice took the police away, and the doctor asked her whether she had fits regularly. She glared angrily at him; her husband had just died, she didn't want to talk about the epilepsy. He patted her hand in reassurance, and asked if she felt able to answer a few questions from the police. She replied that there was nothing wrong with her.

The doctor went into the kitchen, and after a few minutes the police returned. They sat opposite her, and asked questions as to Michael's swimming ability, which she replied was excellent, his state of mind, which she described as relaxed and cheerful. She wished they would stop calling her Mrs Webb. Mrs Webb was Michael's mother, the dreadful Jennifer, and she did not want to be confused with her. She could not bring herself to explain. However, when they asked when she had last seen Michael, she could only say that she could not remember, that she had been awake when he came to bed the previous night, but that she could not recall having seen him since.

When they looked puzzled, she explained about the fit. They continued to look sceptical. They told her that Alice had said that she had raised the alarm that morning on finding her husband gone, and that she, Alice, believed that he had gone out sometime very early that morning. All Laura could say was that she couldn't remember. They asked what she had been doing since she got up, which was after all, two to three hours before the discovery of Mr Webb's body. Again she could not answer.

Had she gone to church with Mr Hansom?

No, she didn't think so, she wasn't a churchgoer.

Did she know what Miss Hansom had been doing in that time? Had they, for example, been out looking for her husband?

Laura shook her head helplessly, and asked what Alice had said about this period of time.

The policewoman referred to her notebook.

'She says that you spent a couple of hours together in your bedroom, talking, and then you had both showered, and were starting to make lunch, when you heard a commotion down by the lake and went to see what had happened.'

Laura shrugged. She could not remember.

'If you were concerned at half past nine, Mrs Webb, why did you spend two hours doing nothing instead of looking for your husband?'

Laura shook her head. The blank was total. If they had told her that only a few minutes had passed, she would have believed them. What she had always dreaded had happened. She had been let down, deserted, by her faculties. She had always expected some unnamed disaster to befall as a result of the epilepsy, but she had never, never imagined something as bad as this.

What if she had drowned Michael. Was it possible? She had been angry enough with him yesterday to commit murder, might she not have done so? Or had Philip drowned him out of jealousy? Or Alice? She remembered the so casual kiss Alice had laid against her cheek on the terrace yesterday. She had known then, or thought she knew, that Alice loved her with a passion that was unsuited to so gentle a kiss.

She said firmly that she was not feeling up to any further

questions, and would like to go to bed. They rose, in unison, gave her conventional expressions of sympathy, and departed, saying that they would return the next day. Laura, trying to control her trembling hands, watched them go, then turned her back firmly to the window and found herself completely at a loss.

*

Getting into the car, the policeman did up his seat belt, waiting for his colleague who seemed to be examining the front of the house with unnecessary interest.

'Well? What do you think?' he asked her.

Ruth Mayhew bit her lip. Sergeant Trent did not generally ask her opinion. In any case, it wasn't their problem. One for CID. Then she realised that CID would be interested in her opinion; she thought Michael Webb had been murdered.

'He was drowned by person or persons unknown,' she said, doing up her seat belt, and thrusting the key into the ignition as though she was stabbing it.

'Why do you think that?' Trent asked, in earnest, as far as she could tell.

'They're all lying. They're covering something up.'

'And you think they're covering for murder?'

'What else?'

Trent raised an eyebrow, he wasn't planning on answering questions, only asking them. Ruth shrugged, turned the key, put the car into gear and stopped thinking about Laura Webb.

Alice knocked at Philip's door, and opened it without waiting for permission. He sat, still soaking wet, on the edge of the bed. His hands knit tight together on his knee, his head down, staring at the carpet. Alice sighed impatiently. She leant against the still open door.

'I want to know what you plan to tell the police.'

He raised his head and stared up at her, bewildered.

'I have nothing to tell them, I was at church.'

'Not at three this morning you weren't, or whenever it was that Michael left your bed.'

Philip winced.

'So, do you plan to tell them he was in your bed? It does give you a motive, in their warped minds.'

'A motive?'

'You don't imagine Michael just drowned, do you?'

'Oh god.'

Philip covered his face with his hands, rubbing them anxiously up and down his cheeks.

'Pull yourself together Philip, we have to think this through. I am assuming you didn't kill him, but the police may not see it like that.'

*

Laura, walking slowly, dazedly, up the stairs overheard Alice's last comment. She stopped, not wanting to go further, suddenly frightened.

'If I tell them I was sleeping with Michael, that would give Laura a motive as well. Jealous wife. She was certainly angry enough.'

'But he was already dead by then,' Alice said impatiently.

'When?' asked Philip, suddenly uncertain of his sister's motives.

Alice opened her mouth to answer, then shut it again. She had no reason for supposing that Michael had died before she was routed from the shower by Laura, unless she thought Laura had killed him. She clung desperately to her anger.

'You don't suspect me?' she asked, trying to sound outraged.

'I don't know what I think. I don't want to think. I haven't even thought through the fact that he's dead, yet.'

Philip's voice shook. Alice sighed, and moved to sit beside him, hugging him gently, despite the wet clothes.

Laura, on the stairs, dismissed Philip as a possible murderer.

Alice, thinking about Laura, wondered whether her histrionics that morning had been cover for the fact that she had already murdered her husband. She wondered whether the passionate embraces they had shared had been to implicate herself, to give her a motive for jealousy and so for murdering her lover's husband. She could not believe it, she told herself, but the doubt was there, sown in the fertile soil of fear.

She wondered whether she dared tell Philip that she too, might be thought to have a motive for murder. But what if he had killed Michael, what if he told the police? She slackened her arms around him.

'I need to talk to Laura,' she said.

Laura stood quickly and slipped down the stairs, returning to the living room.

Alice found her staring out the window. She laid a hand gently on her shoulder, but found it tensed in readiness for her touch.

'Did you really have a fit this morning?'

Laura turned to stare at her in surprise. She had not thought Alice would doubt her. She nodded, not trusting her voice.

'Then you don't remember what we were doing this morning, when the police think we should have been looking for Michael?'

'No.' Laura's voice was husky with a dread the cause of which she could not find.

'Oh.'

Alice looked away uncertainly. How to tell her? And if it was true, then she had been misjudging a woman she thought she loved. So swift to doubt. She swallowed down a fear she had not expected to feel.

'We… you and I, we made love, for nearly two hours. I can't believe you don't remember.'

Alice's last words exploded from her despite her best efforts to keep silent.

Laura laughed, disbelievingly. If only it were true. Was it true? Could it be true? Why would Alice make up something like that? If it was a lie it was too appalling to contemplate. But so was murder. And if it was true? She decided not to think about it.

'And what did we do then?' she asked in a light conversational tone, such as she might have used to an inventive child.

'We had a shower together. And drank some coffee.' Alice stammered over each word. She couldn't credit it. Laura simply didn't believe her. She had not suddenly remembered, she had neither accepted nor denied it, she just refused to believe. What could she think of Alice under these circumstances? She wasn't sure what she thought of herself.

Laura continued to look at Alice in an expectant fashion; then, when she said nothing more, shrugged.

'I don't think I wish to stay here anymore. I think I had better go home. Do you suppose the police will have any objection?'

Alice sat down on the arm of the sofa. She no longer trusted her legs. She shook her head.

'I'll phone them and ask if you like,' she said, defeated.

*

PC Ruth Mayhew had just finished writing up her report when the phone on the desk next to hers rang. Sergeant Trent had gone to lunch, so she answered it.

Alice Hansom's cool voice asked for Sergeant Trent. She recognised her immediately. Ruth was good at voices.

Miss Hansom explained that Mrs Webb was extremely distressed, and wished to be with her family, would there be any objection to her going home?

Ruth rather thought there might be, in the circumstances; however she put Alice Hansom on hold and rang through to the DI who would be handling the case if the post mortem showed what they expected it to. DI Oliver O'Brien did not object, provided the lady made herself available for the inquest, and left a contact address. Ruth relayed this information to her caller, and took down the address where Laura Webb could be contacted. After she had replaced the phone on Simon's desk, she stared at the address for a long time.

*

Alice drove Laura to the station in silence. In a way she was glad. Philip was as much as she could manage at present. But she felt lonely, as she sat behind the wheel of the car and watched Laura walk towards the ticket office. She wanted to run out after her, to grab and shake her and make her believe. She did not want to let her walk away like that, thinking she was crazy or a liar. She had let Anna walk away, let her have her way, even though she knew it was wrong. She had been afraid to make demands, she had let go, and Anna had died. At the door Laura hesitated and looked back, but she did not wave. She vanished into the darkness of the station.

Alice let out the breath she had been holding. She backed the car out of the parking space and turned it awkwardly out into the road, cursing a wayward pedestrian who stepped into her path. Once out of the town she put her foot down and forced the battered vehicle to its fastest speed. It was not fast enough. Even the alarming bends and narrowness of the roads did not test her skill, or divert her attention as she wished. She wanted it to be dangerous. She wanted to be frightened. She wanted anything, anything but this dead dragging pain inside her head.

Abruptly she pulled over into a passing space, turned off the engine, put her head against the steering wheel and cried bitterly. Every time she felt strong enough, or foolish enough, to stop, she found another reason to cry, and began again. Only when a tractor with a wide trailer could not get past her, did she start the engine and roar up the hill, with tears still dripping off her face.

Laura, on the train, stared out of the window and tried not to think. She was too hot. That was safe. She thought how the air-conditioned carriage should be cooler. Cool like the kitchen of the farmhouse. No. She caught sight of water, a river perhaps, and Michael's yellow hair dripped mud in front of her eyes. She closed them. Darkness. Soft darkness, the hum of the air conditioning, the rattle of the wheels, the rustle of the newspaper of the man opposite. She opened her eyes again, it was no good. She would just have to think about it. So she thought.

Saturday night, after the disastrous trip to the stately home. It had rained, hadn't it, and then cleared in the evening, early evening. She had gone to bed early. Michael had stayed up late, talking to Philip. He had come to bed when the rain had started again, torrential; she had felt the temperature drop suddenly. She had gone to sleep, then what?

Then, she supposed, Michael had crept out of their bed, and gone to Philip's. Angry resentment brought a flush to her cheeks. Good. She could still be angry with him, perhaps it wouldn't hurt so much if she were angry. Or perhaps it wouldn't hurt at all, perhaps she was even glad? No, if she thought she might be glad her husband were dead, it was a short step to thinking she could have killed him.

So, no, she would not think that it might not hurt. She wished she had never married him. All those years, safe and yes, happy. And now she felt like a criminal. She did not know if she was a murderer, and there was that other thing she did not know, lurking spider-like in the back of her mind, ready to spring out and ensnare a straying thought.

Alice. She thought about that dream, was it a dream? And Alice saying –

we made love for nearly two hours. And then they had showered together. Well her hair had been wet, hadn't it, so that must be true; unless one or both of them had drowned Michael.

But he might have already been dead when they were making love, if they had been. She wished she could remember, it seemed a waste to have had such knowledge, such experience, and not have the benefit of the memory. Suddenly Laura was shocked at herself, but still, she did wish she knew what it had been like, whether she had enjoyed it, whether Alice had, if it had happened. How could she face Alice again not knowing? She knew she had been cruel, pretending not to believe Alice, not believing Alice. But if Alice had killed Michael – If *she* had killed him, what difference did it make that they had been making love all morning, other than to make matters worse?

And here was London, and the tube to Waterloo to be negotiated and the blessed bustle and rush and confusion, even on a Sunday, for which she was grateful. She could disappear in the London crowd and really not think about anything but the right staircase to the right platform.

*

Catherine Exley was in bed. She was not alone, and she was enjoying herself. It was a hot Sunday, late afternoon, and the sun slid idle fingers across her body in much the same way as the woman beside her.

And then she heard a key turn in the lock. At first she thought she had imagined it; but Marsha, who, despite being twenty-three, still lived at home with her parents and lived in dread of that particular noise, had frozen into horrified stillness.

'Who the hell is that?' she whispered.

Catherine shook her head, and hoped she wasn't about to be burgled. Cautiously she grabbed a dressing gown from the heap of discarded clothes beside the bed. Pulling it on, she tied it tightly around her waist, and picked up the only weapon she could find, an extremely heavy book.

Laura stared in incomprehension at the living room which seemed no longer to be hers. The walls were no longer book lined, the sofa was in a different place, the desk had gone. Posters replaced her carefully framed engravings. She put her suitcase down and opened the door to the flat to check the number on the door. Then a voice said,

'Laura, what are you doing here? I thought I was being burgled.'

She turned to see a young woman in a dressing gown standing at the door to her bedroom. For a moment she did not recognise her.

'Catherine?' she asked stunned, and then realised what she had done. She dissolved into helpless laughter.

Catherine put down her weapon, feeling both relieved and angry. She waited for Laura to stop laughing, but she didn't. Catherine began to be alarmed. Marsha appeared behind her fully dressed, clutching her bag, and looking mutinous. Laura caught sight of her and abruptly stopped laughing.

Oh shit, thought Catherine, despairing at being caught in bed by a woman who was not only her landlord, but her employer.

Laura looked at the two young women standing in the doorway of what had once been her bedroom. She took in the look of embarrassed dread on the face of one, and the look of helpless fury on the face of the other, and recognised, with absolute certainty, what it was that she had interrupted.

'Where's Michael?' Catherine asked, for something to say other than *go away*.

'He's dead,' Laura said. 'And the police seem to think I killed him, and they might be right, I can't remember.'

No, Laura thought, *I can't remember, and I never shall. But it doesn't matter whether I remember, because I know, I do know what I want, if it is still possible*.

*

Monday afternoon: DI Oliver O'Brien read through the post mortem again. He couldn't believe it. Even without interviewing the Webb woman and her friends, he had been convinced this was to become a murder case. There was something fishy about the whole set up. Who goes on their honeymoon with anyone other than their spouse? Not natural.

He rang through to Sergeant Trent, who, despite the fact that the Monday afternoon shift had started twenty minutes before, was not there. Ruth Mayhew answered. *Now*, he thought, *she had been sure too*. It had come off the pages of her report in a wave. She ought to learn to be more objective, at least on paper. Somehow her subjective judgements seemed to blame for his disappointment. He was angry, it was her fault that Michael Webb was not murdered. He told her bluntly that Michael Webb had died, of drowning, probably caused by cramp. Apparently the rain the day before, and then all through the night had lowered the water temperature, and increased the depth, drastically. He had got into difficulties in the unexpectedly cold, deep water, and it had killed him. No foul play, no sign of a struggle, no bruising, nothing. Perhaps she would like to put the grieving friends out of their misery?

Ruth was surprised, but relieved. She was glad that none of the people she had met were murderers. But still she was disappointed that there would be no investigation, no further questioning. She was disappointed that she would not see Laura Webb again. Well, she could at least speak to her. She pulled a file towards her and extracted the phone number. After two rings the phone connected with a hiss. She sighed, an answerphone. A youngish male voice told her that he was not able to take her call. Nor ever would be, she thought, listening to the voice of a dead man.

She left a brief message and rang off. So Laura Webb was not at home. She was not surprised. She had assumed the story about wanting to be with her family was fabricated.

Philip Hansom answered the phone on the third ring, he

had probably been waiting to hear. His relief was palpable, even over the phone. For a moment, as she hung up, Ruth regretted not being able to speak to Laura Webb in person. She shrugged, there was always the inquest. Then she would get the chance to have another look, and persuade herself that this woman was not a murderer. Ruth closed the file, and put it in her out tray.

*

Alice did not get home from her solitary walk until it was almost dark. Philip felt ashamed that he had ever suspected either his sister or Laura of murder. He was also ashamed of his relief. Michael was still dead, and he had loved him, really loved him. But he knew that, despite that love, he had thought he would be happier if Michael did not exist. He was afraid that somehow the thought had caused the accident, that he might have been thinking it at the very moment that Michael had been struggling for his life in the freezing water of the tarn.

Alice, on hearing the news, had cried, and cried. The only time Philip could remember her crying like this before had been when she had finally given up on a close friend who had been addicted to heroin. But she hadn't cried when they heard that Anna had died of an overdose only a few weeks later; she had already done her grieving. He recognised her grief, and its cause. *Poor Alice*, he thought, *never able to quite bring herself to the brink, because of me, because it would be too ridiculous for us both to be gay.*

Alice cried, because she had allowed Laura to walk out of her life. She gave herself up to it. Philip let her cry herself to a stop, then he said very, very softly;

'She is still there, somewhere. Not like Michael. Not like Anna.'

When she looked up at him, he smiled at her surprise.

'Did you think I hadn't noticed?' he asked her. Then he went to find the train timetable.

Alice wiped her eyes. Not like Michael, no. She had not had space to think about Philip's grief. She had seen him only as someone who needed her, when she did not want to be needed. He was right. Laura would not come back here now, whether she knew Michael's death was an accident or not, whether she believed what Alice had told her or not. But nothing between Laura and herself was ended. If she wanted Laura, she must go and find her.

*

Tuesday: Laura finally let herself into her matrimonial home. She had had to steel herself to come back here, and had spent thirty-six hours in a hotel, thinking very carefully about the future, and about Alice.

She pulled the curtains back to let the light in. A light flashed on the answerphone, She pressed the playback button without thinking.

Michael's voice startled her.

Hello, I'm sorry we are not able to take your call –

Laura closed her eyes. Muddy water streamed down his back.

Jennifer Webb, clearly in tears, asking her to phone as soon as she got home. The police must have got in touch with her. Laura found she could feel sorry for Michael's mother, as she did not feel sorry for herself.

A young woman's voice.

Hello, this is PC Ruth Mayhew from Lakes Police. I just wanted you to know that the P.M. seems to indicate that your husband's death was an accident. Um. I hope you are feeling better. The inquest has been set for next Wednesday. Bye.

Laura wanted to laugh. The little red-haired policewoman, tongue-tied at having to ring the grieving widow. *She hopes I am feeling better. Sweet.* And then she took in the import of the message. *Accident. Dear god, an accident.* She found herself trembling with relief, needing a drink so badly that she stumbled over her suitcase. She found the gin, poured herself a generous measure, breathing in the fumes before adding a small amount of tonic. She drank it quickly, reminded of the first time she had drunk gin in this room. She did not want to be reminded. She poured another, put the answerphone back on. Again, Michael's voice.

'Shut up,' she told him, angry, desperate. She took off her shoes, and lay on the sofa, gin bottle within reach. Intending to get very drunk.

But she did not get drunk. The doorbell rang.

For a moment she quailed before the thought that the police had changed their minds. But no, it wasn't possible. The doorbell rang again, insistently.

'Go away,' she said, under her breath.

Alice, walking up the stairs, had listened to her heart yammering; trying to tell her to turn round, to walk away, not to lay herself open to Laura's refusal, her scorn. She had had to force her legs to move, to step up, again and again. Her hand on the rail was sweaty. She was not going to let this one slip away. If she was going to lose, she would go down fighting.

When Laura did not answer the door, the feeling of anticlimax was more than she could bear. She pushed the bell again, long and hard. She could hear her in there, knocking things over. Alice allowed her anger just a little rein. She hit the door with the heel of her hand, once. The door made a satisfying noise, so she did it again. And again.

Laura had had enough of the fear that had been eating her for so long. She was not going to be afraid of whoever was hitting her door. She got to her feet, slamming the glass down on the table so that the liquid spilled. Leaping the suitcase still blocking the way, she flung the door open.

Alice looked at her, trying to gauge Laura's mood. She was half-afraid the door would be slammed in her face. But it wasn't.

Laura swayed slightly on her feet, she did not seem to have understood that Alice was there. Then, very slowly, she smiled.

Laura said nothing, not knowing what to say. This woman, who loved her, who had made love to her; had suspected her of murder. She had, in turn loved, made love, suspected. But here Alice was, on her doorstep, not knowing that she no longer doubted her. Taking risks. So she smiled. If she was ever to put her life back together, she must take risks, as she had never done in her life before. Laura knew she could do it. She knew that she welcomed the chance that she was being offered. There would be no more safety, no more planning. Nothing would ever be the same again.

The phone rang. Two rings, then the click and whirr as the answerphone prepared itself. Laura couldn't stand it, not again, not now. She leaped for the plug, and wrenched it out of the socket. Michael's voice slurred deepened, and stopped. Alice had not come all the way from Kendal on a milk train to hesitate. She pulled the door shut behind her.

'The police have decided it was an accident,' she said quickly, taking Laura's shaking hands in hers.

'I know,' Laura said, clinging to her friend, feeling the warmth of her hands. She did not want to talk about Michael. He was dead, gone. Alice was alive, here. Very alive, very close, warm and –

'I'm sorry,' Laura said, trying to find a way to break the deadlock between them.'I'm sorry I didn't believe you.'

Alice suddenly didn't mind very much that Laura hadn't believed her. Something about the way she had pulled the answerphone plug, the ruthlessness, the anger, let her know that things had changed in the last forty-eight hours; Laura believed her now. More than that, Laura wanted to believe her. That was enough.

ABOUT THE AUTHOR

Cherry Potts lives in London with her life partner and two very spoilt cats.

She is the author of two collections of short stories: *Mosaic of Air,* and *Tales Told Before Cockcrow* (OnlyWomen Press), a photographic diary of a community opera *The Blackheath Onegin* (Curved Air Press), and she has had several stories in anthologies. She is has completed a lesbian fantasy epic, and is currently working on a science fiction novel based on the title story of *Mosaic of Air*, her next collection and a timeslip-young-adult novel. She also runs workshops for writers exploring NLP (Neurolinguistic programming) approaches to language and characterisation.

Cherry is the owner of Arachne Press, editor of *Stations* and co-editor of *London Lies, Lovers' Lies* and *Weird Lies.*

Cherry sings for fun with several community choirs including *Vocal Chords* and *Blackheath Halls Chorus*, and a small group, *Summer All Year Long*. She has a burning ambition to write an opera.

MORE BOOKS FROM ARACHNE PRESS

London Lies, ISBN: 978-1-909208-00-1 is our first Liars' League showcase.

Moving from 1930s Camden to a Royal Wedding 'riot', via football fights, office steeplechases and awkward dates in art galleries, *London Lies* is a bizarre, funny, moving and sometimes unnerving glimpse into the secret life of the city we all love and know – or do we?

Stations, ISBN: 978-1-909208-01-8 is a collection of stories connected by the Overground line in East and South London.

From tigers in a South London suburb to retired police inspectors investigating a series of train-based thefts, from collectors of poets at Shadwell to life-changing decisions in Canonbury, by way of an art installation that defies the boundaries of a gallery, *Stations* takes a sideways look through the steamed up windows of the Overground train, at life as it is lived beside the rails.

A story for every station from New Cross, Crystal Palace, and West Croydon at the Southern extremes of the line, all the way to Highbury & Islington.

Lovers' Lies ISBN: 978-1-909208-02-5 is our second collaboration with Liars' League bringing the freshness, wit, imagination and passion of their authors to stories of love: this book is for romantic cynics and cynical romantics.

Love changes everything – it makes cheese take centre stage, it brings people back from wars, it clears your ears, it takes a leap into the unknown.

Old love, cold love, true love, new love, dead love, we're

through love – making babies and making whoopee, disappointment and contentment, playing at home, playing away or just playing; missed chances and new romances: everything from first conversation to last breath, strange journeys and stranger destinations.

Weird Lies ISBN: 978-1-909208-10-0

More than twenty stories varying in style from tales not out of place in *One Thousand and One Nights,* to the completely bemusing.

Discover mirrors that predict imminent events and museums where your personal future life is exhibited in the kind of ephemeral objects that might normally find their way into a dustbin.

Meet tadpoles, lazy assassins, and assiduous poisoners, observe deals with the devil and workplace stress taken to its logical conclusion.

Heroes, villains, and animals – anything and anyone – cursed travellers, persistent dreamers, aliens, robots, even ice could provide the twist in the tale.

EVENTS

Arachne Press is enthusiastic about live literature and makes an effort to present our books through readings. If you run a bookshop, a literature festival or any other kind of literature venue, get in touch, we'd love to talk to you.

WORKSHOPS

Arachne Press offers writing workshops, available as one-off's or a series of linked events, suitable for writers' groups, literature festivals, evening classes – if you are interested, please let us know.

www.arachnepress.com